The Second Coffeyville Bank Raid

When Jean Pierre Boudreaux leaves New Orleans with three companions he is wanted for a brutal murder he swears he did not commit. Six months later he plans a one-off bank robbery that will give him the money to start a new life. The bank is the Coffeyville First National – the scene of the Daltons' infamous robbery attempt.

Boudreaux's raid secures him the money but his companions are captured. When his daring rescue attempt fails, Boudreaux finds himself hunted by two Pinkerton operatives. He then discovers that the enigmatic Dom Ramés, now mysteriously free, is planning a double-cross.

With blonde Alice LaClaire at his side, Boudreaux battles on through fire and gun-smoke, but it is not until the final bloody climax that he finds out if he is to remain a wanted killer or become a free man.

The Second Coffeyville Bank Raid

Matt Laidlaw

A Black Horse Western

ROBERT HALE · LONDON

ISBN 978-0-7090-8874-5

Robert Hale Limited
Clerkenwell House
Clerkenwell Green
London EC1R 0HT

www.halebooks.com

Typeset by
Derek Doyle & Associates, Shaw Heath
Printed and bound in Great Britain by
CPI Antony Rowe, Chippenham and Eastbourne

PROLOGUE

July 1893

The office was a fug of cigar smoke, the afternoon sun slanting through the window. The eyes of the man sitting in the swivel chair were bright and intelligent: James McParland leaned back and laced his fingers across his substantial girth. As the dark eyes began to twinkle, the look on his plump, moustachioed face became one of immense satisfaction.

'It's been six months,' he said. 'Now, out of the blue, there's been a sighting.'

Sitting across the desk from the superintendent of the Pinkerton National Detective Agency's western operations, Jim Gatlin and Charlie Pine exchanged glances. Both were Pinkerton operatives.* Gatlin had been taken on after his excellent investigative work tracking criminal Nathan Hood to the town of Cedar Creek in Wyoming. Hood had framed Gatlin for a crime he did not commit. Gatlin served

* See *The Night Riders*, Robert Hale 2006

THE SECOND COFFEYVILLE BANK RAID

his time, then went after Hood. He met Pine in Cedar Creek. After Hood's arrest, at Pine's invitation Gatlin had ridden south with him to the Pinkertons' Denver office. Since then he had been working out of that office, often with Charlie Pine; they made an excellent team, and were difficult to beat.

'A sighting of who, and where?' Gatlin said now.

'Man called Waltz. A prospector spotted him in the foothills of the Superstition Mountains—'

'Cut it out, James,' Charlie Pine said. He shook his head as he looked at Gatlin. 'He's pulling your leg. Waltz is supposed to be the feller who owned the Lost Dutchman Mine in Arizona. He died in Phoenix a couple of years ago.'

McParland was chuckling.

'All right, all right, I am joking, but it's with a serious intent. I expect my agents to be alert, aware of subtle nuances in a man's tone or manner of delivery that point to the veracity or otherwise of what he's saying.' He grinned as Gatlin looked sideways at Charlie Pine and rolled his eyes, then slammed his palms on the desk. 'But getting down to the serious business, has either of you heard of Jean Pierre Boudreaux?'

'New Orleans, 1892,' Pine said at once. 'An intruder broke into living quarters above a saloon on Bourbon Street. The owner was an old man. He must have heard something and woke up. There was a fight. The intruder had a knife. He cut the owner's throat, then must have seen the old man's wife watching him and he went back. The second time he used the knife he cut that woman's neck clear through to the bone.'

'Where does this Boudreaux come in? You saying he's

the killer?'

'Positive identification.'

'And after twelve months there's been a sighting?' Gatlin said.

McParland nodded. 'Yep. The man's been spotted by a marshal name of Miller.'

'What did he do, break out of jail?'

'He was never caught,' McParland said.

'If the owner and his wife were murdered, they couldn't talk. How did the law figure out it was Boudreaux?'

'He was identified by his fingerprints.'

'Whoa, now, surely that's newfangled stuff, not yet been proved accurate enough to be trusted?' Charlie Pine said.

McParland looked smug. 'You men are supposed to keep up with developments in investigative techniques. The English began using fingerprints in India way back in '58. Gilbert Thompson of the Geological Survey in New Mexico used his own thumb print on a document to prevent forgery. That was in '82. You'll also find 'em used in a fiction book by Mark Twain. But that double murder in New Orleans in '92 was fact. There was another interesting case only last year. A woman called Frances Rojas murdered her two sons, then cut her own throat to escape suspicion.'

'Jesus,' Jim Gatlin said softly.

'She didn't get away. A feller called Juan Vucetich identified her using a bloody palm print she left on a door post.'

'Is that what Boudreaux did?' Charlie Pine said, leaning forward.

'Exactly. Also, he stole a heap of money. And some kind

7

of an icon. An amulet the male victim wore around his neck on a leather thong. According to his neighbours, the old feller brought it with him from Russia.'

Pine frowned. 'But if Boudreaux had any sense at all, he would have hightailed. With him gone, how would anyone know whose print that was?'

'The intruder was seen leaving the building and identified as Boudreaux by a casual acquaintance who was passing at the time. Once they had a name, and a description, all they had to do was get prints from where Boudreaux lived, and compare. The prints at the murder scene matched. They had their killer.'

'Only they didn't,' Gatlin pointed out. 'And six months later he's still on the loose.'

'And back in business,' McParland said. 'That sighting I mentioned was in the town of Coffeyville. Miller's the new town marshal, and he makes it his business to look through Wanted dodgers, memorize details and faces. He spotted the man he believes to be Boudreaux a week ago. In town. Acting suspicious.'

'But he didn't arrest him?'

'Why take one man when you might get the chance at a whole bunch of villains? Boudreaux was practically rubbing his hands while looking across the street at the bank. Miller's allowed him some rope.'

'So what do we do?'

'Miller's sitting back awaiting developments,' McParland said. 'I want you to do the same, but not here. Book yourself seats on the Atchison, Topeka & Santa Fe. That'll take you as far as Arkansas City. If there's no branch line to Coffeyville, you'll be left with a sixty-mile ride.'

'And then?'

McParland's grin was wolfish.

'Book yourself into the hotel, wait, and watch. The Pinkertons have been looking for Boudreaux for twelve months. No small town lawman's going to snatch that feller from under our noses.'

PART ONE

ONE

It was Dom Ramés who, late that evening, spotted the rider on the skyline. Tired of lying close to the fire with his head on his hard saddle, smoking a chain of cigarettes and listening to the two women jabbering endlessly about the life they had left behind in New Orleans, he walked down the slope to the river-bank, flicked his cigarette and watched it hiss into flat waters that were reflecting the fiery western skies. When he looked up, Jean Pierre Boudreaux was a quarter-mile away, dropping off the ridge and into the gold-tinted shadows as he worked his big bay down the steep, twisting track through the tangled mesquite. It took Boudreaux another five minutes to make it to the bottom of the hill and ride across the grassy basin on the Elk River where the group had been camping for the past three days. When he reached Ramés and swung down from the saddle he was grinning all over his face.

'Break out the whiskey, Dom. I've got me an idea so original it'll make us famous throughout the West,' he said, and he dug into his saddle-bag and brought out a yellowing newspaper which he held aloft and brandished

13

in the fading light.

By this time Alice and Caroline had come jogging down from the camp-fire. They both heard Boudreaux's announcement. Alice was not slow to express her disbelief.

'What makes me think I've heard that before, Jean Pierre?' she said, hands on hips, head cocked. 'Could it be because this is where your big ideas have brought us? Middle of nowhere, with nowhere left to go?'

'If they have, then you've been with me all the way of your own free will, my lovely, so I must be doing something right. Of course, if you decided to walk away now that'd leave us with a better split when the money comes rolling in. . . .'

He straightened, stripped the rig from the bay and began walking up the slope. Broad-shouldered, with hair as shiny and black as coal oil beneath a faded Stetson and with a six-gun tied low on each thigh, he managed to put a swagger into his walk despite the slope and the weight of the saddle.

They watched him go, followed more slowly and came together around the fire under the trees: Jean Pierre Boudreaux, Dom Ramés, Alice LaClaire and Caroline Chauvin. Ramés threw fresh logs on the dying embers. Damp wood hissed. Sparks ascended like fireflies. He got the coffee going, the blackened pot dangling over the fire from sticks he'd rigged. Grinning, Boudreaux stepped around the fire, took the whiskey bottle from Ramés's saddle-bag and splashed a generous measure into four tin cups. When the coffee was ready, he watched Ramés top up the cups with the steaming black java.

Sitting cross-legged with the now dancing flames

lighting the hard planes of his face and glinting in his dark eyes, Boudreaux lifted his mug high.

'Here's to us,' he said, 'and the big time.'

Blonde Alice LaClaire was stretched out with her hands laced behind her head. She was 25 years old, and as slim as a willow wand in blue denim pants and shirt.

She raised her cup to Boudreaux.

'Here's to us, and one more wild scheme that from past experience I guarantee will come to nothing,' she said.

'You're wrong. So far we've got nowhere because we've been operating in an honest way, on the right side of the law. Trouble is, according to the law in New Orleans I've been on the wrong side ever since they discovered those bodies.'

'If you'd stayed to fight your case, I'm sure you'd have won,' Alice said. 'You discovered that poor old couple. You touched them, got blood on your hands—'

'What makes you so sure that's how it happened?' Ramés said.

'I just know, that's all. Pierre's not a killer.'

'We all have secrets. Maybe that's his.'

'No. He was in that room and he heard someone coming and he panicked, and ran.' She looked at Boudreaux and shook her head. 'Money was stolen, and you haven't got it – right, Pierre? You know you should have stayed, told the truth.'

'But I didn't,' Boudreaux said.

'And you've been on the run ever since.'

'Six months. Way too late to go back. Nobody's going to listen to me now.'

The flat finality in those words revealed bitterness,

15

regret, but also resignation and a desire to put the past behind him. For a moment a look of pain crossed his face. Then it was wiped away as he lifted his head high, and his smile was roguish when he looked at Alice.

'My words would fall on deaf ears if I pleaded innocent,' he said, 'but if people won't listen to the truth then maybe I should enter into the spirit of things, play out the role they've assigned to me.'

Alice raised her eyebrows to Caroline and Ramés, then cocked her head at Boudreaux, her blue eyes troubled.

'So what are we going to do that's unlawful, Jean Pierre? Rob a bank?'

'That's it,' he said, and there was a new serenity in his voice. 'Alice, if I'm to get the money I need to make a fresh start, then that's exactly what we're going to have to do.'

Dusk had fallen swiftly and a crescent moon floated above a veil of cloud. The western hills were an indistinct smudge spanning the horizon and backed by a fading, ruddy glow. Firelight flickered on overhanging branches, and on the faces of the three people sitting close to the flames.

Caroline Chauvin was sitting just outside the warm circle of light. She was the same age as Alice, but dark, sulky, and a thinker. Her dark hair was worn long and loose. A solid figure in fringed leather pants and a loose butternut Confederate shirt, she wore a six-gun butt-forward in a holster suspended from her broad leather belt and resting on her shapely left hip.

'The fellers running Wichita's bank must be quaking in

their boots,' she said. 'They know you're comin' back, Jean Pierre?'

'My plans have got nothing to do with Wichita,' Boudreaux said. 'They do owe a lot to some boys by the name of Dalton who set out to rob two banks in Coffeyville.'

Dom Ramés was up on his feet and prowling restlessly with the tin cup of laced coffee in his hand. He was a very tall man with a lean frame. His clothing was always black and tight-fitting, the gun he carried in a pared-down holster a Colt Peacemaker. In the thin moonlight he was a sinister, shifting shadow.

He stopped at Boudreaux's words, and swung to face him.

'October 5th, last year,' he said. 'That raid finished the Daltons. You base all your ideas on losers?'

'I learn from mistakes made by others,' Boudreaux said.

Alice frowned.

'Learn what, Jean Pierre? Choice ways of losin'?'

But Boudreaux was smiling and biding his time, riding the cheap jibes like a veteran prize fighter. He knew the idea that had hit him that morning while sitting in a Wichita eating-house with two newspapers spread across the table – one old, one new – was not a loser, but a winner. The Daltons' stupidity, which became clear as he read the report of the Coffeyville raid, had filled him with scorn; when the idea for the perfect bank robbery popped up out of the blue, he had been dumbfounded.

'It didn't finish them,' he said, his mind busy as he looked at Ramés. 'Grat and Bob are dead, yes, but Emmett

17

Dalton's still alive, and so's Bill.'

'Emmett's in jail. Bill Dalton wasn't at Coffeyville,' Ramés said.

'No. He's riding with Bill Doolin's Wild Bunch.'

'Proving what?'

'In October last year, Doolin's bunch robbed the Ford County Bank in Spearville. If they can do it and get away—'

'Wasn't O.L. Yantis later gunned down by lawmen at his sister's ranch?'

'OK, but it took 'em thirty days to find him. My point is, Doolin and his boys made it out of the bank, and out of town. Since then – last month – they've robbed a train at Cimarron. Doolin was wounded, but again they got away. If they can do it, we can do it.'

'With respect, Jean Pierre,' Alice LaClaire said, 'you're not Bill Doolin and, like Caroline, I happen to be a female woman.'

'Damn right, on both counts,' Boudreaux said fiercely. 'And because you're right, because I'm not Doolin and you're a woman, we're going to raid the Coffeyville's First National Bank, just like the Daltons. They failed. We'll do it successfully, without bloodshed—'

'You can't guarantee that,' Ramés cut in. 'You say you're innocent of those New Orleans killings, but an evil reputation's been tacked to your back. If you're spotted, recognized, we'll be caught in a hail of gunfire, hunted down like dogs if we make it out of town.'

'You finished?'

'I've said my piece. Alice was talking sense. Maybe you should go back to New Orleans and sort out that mess. Confront the authorities, tell them your story and clear your name. Or is it that you're scared of taking that step because you could end up with a noose around your neck?'

He was staring hard at Boudreaux, naked challenge in his eyes, and for a few brief moments Boudreaux wondered what the hell the man in black was trying to do. What good, he wondered, would it do Ramés if he, Boudreaux, was convicted of a double murder?

Then Ramés shook his head, met Boudreaux's fierce gaze and grinned crookedly. 'All right, I'm not getting through to you, but I've said my piece. I think this raid is a bad idea, so now you know where we stand.'

'On the threshold of a fortune,' Boudreaux said. 'That's where we all stand. And you're wrong, there is a way back. This raid offers us the way back – offers me the way back.'

'Are you saying you're forced into this?' Alice said. 'That there's no other way?'

Her eyes were still troubled, but now there was compassion there too. For a moment it was as if the two of them were alone, their locked gaze and the thoughts that seemed to pass between them excluding all others. Then Boudreaux broke the spell. He did it by continuing as if there had been no interruption, his eyes reproving because the answer was there if only she had waited.

'It's a one off, something I don't intend ever to repeat. And we'll do it like I said, without bloodshed, without risk, because the way I've got this planned nobody outside the bank manager's office will know a robbery's taken place until we're clear of town and ten miles into the hills.'

*

19

Later that evening, Jean Pierre Boudreaux sat at the camp-fire with Alice LaClaire. They were enclosed within the warm circle of the firelight. Around them the soft sounds of the night were weaving their magic spell, and Alice's eyelids were drooping.

'I didn't mean that,' Boudreaux said softly. 'About us splitting three ways if you walked out on us. I know you won't do that. You've stuck with me so far—'

'More than that. It was me told you, after that bad thing happened, the only thing for it was to leave New Orleans.'

'I know. And you were right. And now I've got the chance to turn everything around.'

'By doing something bad yourself?'

'A one off. The way I've planned it, nobody gets hurt. When it's over, Caroline and Dom can go their separate ways, we can disappear. Go where you want to go, do what you want to do—'

'I'm scared, Jean Pierre.'

'I was scared, back in New Orleans, and you showed me the way out. Now it's my turn.'

'I'm scared in more ways than one. I can't figure Dom, and I don't think I trust him. I know Caroline doesn't like him one bit. When he was talking before it was almost as if he wanted you to return to New Orleans – yet he must know if you did that you'd be hanged for a double murder.'

'Leave Dom Ramés to me. I must admit I don't know what he's playing at, but I'm confident I can handle anything that skinny feller cares to dish up.'

He dropped his tin cup by the glowing embers at the edge of the fire, walked over to the slim blonde and bent to place a tender kiss on her forehead.

'Sweet dreams, Alice,' he said gruffly.

When he rolled himself in his blankets under the trees she was still sitting at the edge of the fire, staring into the darkness.

TWO

The immaculate top-buggy was pulled by a well-groomed chestnut mare with a sheen to her coat and a spring in her step. The driver was a man who sat almost regally erect in his dark suit, dove-grey Stetson and polished, tooled-leather boots. He wore a six-gun in a belt holster, visible under the jacket – but, in the West, that was not unusual. Alongside him a young woman with an aloof air about her wore a plain navy-blue dress, a wrap draped across her shoulders and a hat of matching colour. A veil as fine as gossamer was swept back from her face. The hem of her dress, caught by the breeze, gave onlookers a discreet view of slender ankles as the buggy effortlessly negotiated the ruts of Coffeyville's main street and the plaza and pulled up alongside the First National Bank.

It was 9.15 in the morning. Already the town was bustling. People on foot hurried to and fro between the various commercial establishments. Dust rose in choking clouds as riders and wagons from outlying ranches and farms vied for space in the crowded streets.

'Bear in mind,' Boudreaux said out of the side of his

mouth, 'those people watching us are interested, but they're not suspicious. Goddammit, dressed the way we are, they're *expecting* us to walk into the bank.'

'Just keep praying my legs don't give way,' said Alice LaClaire. 'I have to tell you, this is the first bank I've ever robbed, and that big man over there watching us is wearing a badge.'

'Give him a sweet smile,' Boudreaux said, and he set the brake and looped the lines before climbing down and walking round the buggy to help Alice down from her seat. On the way, and while assisting her, he managed to cast his eyes in the direction she'd indicated. Sure enough, a lawman of some kind was standing on the edge of a plank walk, paying a lot of attention to the top-buggy and its occupants.

Keep cool, Boudreaux thought. You've thought this through and there's not a damn thing can go wrong.

The bank, when they entered, was a place of calm after the clamour of the street. Only two customers were being served. An unoccupied senior cashier caught Boudreaux's eye, cast an approving eye over the couple's attire and hurried round the counter to greet them.

'Good morning, sir, madam. Can I be of assistance?'

'My name is John Savage,' Boudreaux said. 'My wife and I have taken over the Burnham property some miles to the north. This bank was recommended to us.'

Made up names – but they sounded important, and who the hell would know?

The cashier dipped his head, glanced with speculation at the leather Gladstone bag Boudreaux was carrying.

'And how can we help you today, Mr Savage?'

Boudreaux pursed his lips.

'Quite a large sum of money is involved,' he said. 'I need your manager's personal attention in this matter.'

'Unfortunately, unless we know the exact nature of any transaction it's not our usual policy—'

'I seem to recall it was this bank that was recommended,' Boudreaux said, deliberately frowning, 'but it's quite possible it was the one directly across the plaza – isn't that the Condon Bank?'

The cashier's manner changed from officious to obsequious. Thirty seconds later, Boudreaux and Alice were ushered into the First National's manager's office. Boudreaux placed the Gladstone bag close to Alice's shiny black shoes. He heard the door click shut behind them. On the other side of an enormous oak desk the manager was on his feet. He was a thin man with greasy grey hair. His smile was tentative. He started around the desk.

'My dear Mr Savage, Mrs Savage—'

Boudreaux said, 'Go back, sit down, and keep your hands flat on the desk.'

From the Gladstone bag, Alice pulled out a Colt .45, cocked it and pointed it at the manager's belly.

The manager's face went white. Suddenly there was a sheen of sweat on his pale forehead. He collapsed into his seat.

'Listen carefully,' Boudreaux said. 'When I give the order you'll walk to the door and open it. You will call your chief cashier. You will tell him that you have spoken to Mr and Mrs Savage, and have agreed a loan of ten thousand dollars, five thousand of which must be available immediately. He is to bring that amount to your office.'

'He won't buy it,' the manager said hoarsely.

'Tell him we've been exchanging letters of a business nature. This loan was arranged a month ago, for completion it required our presence, our signatures.'

'That's not what's going to bother him.' The manager was shaking his head. 'There are too many memories of the raid by the Dalton gang, too much grief—'

'He'll see nothing to ruffle his feathers,' Boudreaux cut in. 'The door will be open, my wife and I will be sitting in front of your desk, you'll have a smile on your face and I'll be conversing with you and smoking one of your cigars.'

Boudreaux reached over, took a fat cigar from a humidor and grinned at the manager.

'What he won't see,' he went on inexorably, 'is that six-gun Mrs Savage will be holding under her wrap. He won't see it, but you'll know it's there and my guess is under the smooth exterior you're going to show him, you'll be shaking in your boots. Because, Mr Manager, you know damn well what will happen if you put a foot wrong.'

'Suppose that works,' the manager said, taking out a handkerchief with a hand that trembled and mopping his face. 'Suppose he brings the money, I hand it to you, you put it in that bag – what then? You'll never get away. You might as well give yourselves up now, prevent more senseless shooting, more bloodshed.'

'Shut up,' Boudreaux said.

The manager's mouth closed. His weak chin was quivering.

'Now go to the door. Call your chief cashier. Tell him what to do.'

It took no more than five minutes for the cashier to be

summoned, depart with his instructions and return with the money. Which was fine with Boudreaux. On the first occasion the manager was at the door to meet him. Boudreaux and Alice were sitting in leather chairs in front of his desk. It was all, Boudreaux figured, running like clockwork.

But between that cosy scene and the cashier's return, something happened that just about stopped Boudreaux's heart. He was sitting puffing at the cigar while watching the manager squirm when there was a loud rapping on the door. Before the manager could open his mouth, the door swung open.

In stepped the burly lawman both Boudreaux and Alice had noticed giving them the eye from across the street. Boudreaux saw Alice bite her lip. In her lap, under the wrap, the hidden six-gun seemed to quiver.

Maybe, Boudreaux thought wildly, if that feller notices he'll think she's cold, or nervous, or—

'Frank,' the lawman said by way of greeting, his cold eyes taking in the visitors' every detail. 'Everything all right in here?'

Jesus Christ, Boudreaux thought, how's he going to reply? And if he says the wrong thing, what's Alice going to do? Plug him and the marshal both – or fall down in a faint?

'Everything's going very well, thank you, Marshall,' the manager said in a voice that was neither steady nor shaky but, Boudreaux judged with vast relief, just plain ordinary.

And the lawman tipped his hat, and was gone.

A couple of minutes later the cashier returned. The manager was seated behind his desk, and he and

26

Boudreaux appeared to be conversing. They were. Boudreaux was giving him his final instructions.

The cashier's arms were occupied with the load he was carrying. He'd used his shoulder to push the door open. Now he strode across the room and dumped the banknotes on the desk.

'One moment, Johnson,' the manager said, as the cashier turned to leave. 'Mr and Mrs Savage will be departing very soon. When they do, please make sure I'm not disturbed. I need at least an hour to catch up with some paperwork. One hour – do you understand?'

The cashier, a sour look on his face, nodded and left the office.

'See how easy that was?' Boudreaux said, puffing a cloud of blue smoke from the big cigar. 'We're almost there, almost finished.'

'I still say you'll never get away,' the manager said. 'They won't disturb me, they know me too well, but what's to stop me walking out of here the minute you're gone—?'

He broke off. Alice had opened the Gladstone bag. She reached inside and brought out a bundle of rawhide thongs and placed them on the desk.

'That's to stop you,' Boudreaux said, and he winked. 'And, by the way, in case you're wondering if Savage is the name you should give them when you're being questioned, it's not. If anyone's interested, you can tell them this is the work of the Doolin gang. The Dalton boys made a mess of things, Bill Doolin figured we could do better. Seems he was right.'

As intended, that crude lie caused all remaining colour

to drain from the manager's face. He closed his eyes, his throat working as he swallowed. Within minutes he was bound and gagged and lying on the floor behind the desk. Swiftly, Boudreaux scooped the money from the desk straight into the Gladstone bag.

When he closed the bag and looked across the desk he realized the room had another door. It was in the back wall, behind the desk, and so hard had Boudreaux been concentrating on the precise execution of his plan to rob the bank, he had failed to notice it. But so what? Did it matter? If it was another way out, it was of no use to him; their escape was arranged, and by a different route. More likely, he thought, it was the door to a storeroom for bank stationery, documents – and with a shrug he decided it was of little importance.

'That'll delay them some more,' he said to Alice, jerking his thumb at the mysterious door. 'They can't see him where he is, trussed up behind the desk. If that door's closed they'll maybe think he's in there, take a while chewing their nails because they're too damn scared to disturb him.'

'I'll be chewing my nails if we don't get out of here,' Alice said. 'Christ, Jean Pierre, when that marshal walked in I damn near wet myself.'

'You'd better brace up, girl. The minute we walk out of here, all eyes will be on us.'

Boudreaux's heart was pounding. The blood was singing in his veins. Almost there. If he pulled this off he'd make those Dalton boys – the ones still alive – look like pathetic blunderers. He was unable to suppress a grin of triumph as, carrying the heavy Gladstone bag, he opened the door and let Alice through.

Holding the door ajar, he turned back and spoke to the empty office.

'Thank you, sir,' he called in his gravest tones. 'You've been a great help to us. In appreciation we'll make sure your head office hears from us and learns of your efficient way of doing business.'

Then he banged the door shut and followed Alice.

The room was crowded. Men and women were at the counter, waiting in line, too involved with their own financial affairs to pay much attention to Boudreaux and Alice. Gently they pushed their way through, politely murmuring apologies, smiling at people who abstractedly looked straight through them. They reached the door; stepped outside into bright sunlight and hustle and bustle.

'We made it – didn't we?' Alice LaClaire said softly, as Boudreaux helped her into the top-buggy.

'Damn right we did,' he answered.

They had not ten miles to go in the top-buggy, but just 200 yards. When Boudreaux flicked his whip to urge the harness horse away from the bank, the buggy was almost lost among the wagons and horses and billowing dust. He drove without haste, touched his forefinger to the brim of his Stetson when he saw the now familiar figure of the burly marshal watching from the plank walk, then turned away to hide a grin. In such a manner they reached the chosen side street – little more than a narrow alley. He turned into it – an insignificant buggy on a busy day in a Kansas town, the direction it was taking unnoticed or quickly forgotten – and drove up the slope between the raw timber walls of the buildings on either side, his eyes searching for the patch of waste ground.

There!

Elated, knowing nothing could stop them now, Boudreaux swung onto the rutted earth and pulled the rocking buggy to a halt.

Dom Ramés was there, with Caroline Chauvin. In addition to his six-gun, Ramés was carrying a shotgun. Caroline had her six gun butt forward on her left hip. They were anxiously watching Boudreaux and Alice La Claire. Four saddled horses were waiting patiently.

'Let's go,' Ramés said.

Swiftly, he and Caroline mounted two of the horses as Boudreaux leaped down from the top-buggy and grabbed the heavy Gladstone bag. Alice was already down and running for one of the two remaining horses, her ladylike manner forgotten as she hiked her skirts high. She flung herself into the saddle, spun the horse and watched with impatience as Jean Pierre transferred the cash from Gladstone-bag to saddle-bag then sent the empty bag tumbling to join the rubbish littering the open space.

'Come on, come on,' Ramés yelled, holding his horse on tight reins as it backed and turned, tossing its head.

'Stop worrying,' Boudreaux said. He was laughing as he stepped up into the saddle and turned the horse to join the others. 'Ask Alice. The authorities won't be looking for us for that bank job, not now, not ever. When that dumb bank manager's spilling his story, he's going to tell them it was a couple of members of the Doolin gang who just walked in and robbed his bank.'

Ramés looked back, his face suddenly twisted with fury.

'If you told him that we owe you some thanks, Jean

Pierre. Your quick thinking means we'll not only have lawmen hunting us down like a pack of rabid dogs, thanks to you the whole of the Doolin gang will now be baying for our blood.'

'You're frightened of your own shadow, Dom,' Boudreaux yelled.

With a quick grin and a wink at Alice and Caroline he spurred his horse past them, riding close enough to Ramés to give him a friendly slap on the back as he rushed by. He swung off the waste ground and into the alley, turned up the slope away from town – and pulled his horse to a skidding, rearing halt.

The way out at the top of the alley was blocked by two silent, menacing riders. They were carrying rifles, or shotguns.

Boudreaux's mouth went dry. The blood singing in his veins turned ice cold. He hauled on the reins and spun his mount on a dime. Ramés and the two women, coming hard off the waste ground, had no time to draw rein or get out of his way. Suddenly there was a tangle of squealing, snorting horses, lashing hoofs, cursing riders. From the centre of the chaos, fighting to stay in the saddle, Boudreaux looked over heads towards the end of the alley that opened onto Coffeyville's main street.

It was blocked. Two riders were sitting motionless on their horses, guarding the entrance. They, too, had rifles resting across their thighs.

THREE

'No way out,' Boudreaux said. 'We're trapped.'

'Oh, Jesus,' Alice LaClaire said tautly, 'and me in my best party frock.'

Caroline's short laugh was chilling. 'I'm dressed for a getaway,' she said, 'but that's no help if there's nowhere to go.'

'Your idea sounded good,' Ramés said to Boudreaux. 'Where we went wrong was not thinking it through.'

'What's that mean?'

'The Dalton raid taught this town a lesson. We should have realized it'd be difficult to fool them a second time.'

'They weren't fooled the first time,' Caroline said. 'The Daltons didn't make it.'

'So what now?' Alice said. 'I hate to interrupt, but those strong, silent fellers are closing in and they don't look friendly.'

Boudreaux was nodding, chewing his lip, his eyes constantly shifting from one end of the alley to the other.

'We could try blasting a way through – any direction you choose – but there's likely to be others waiting for us when we burst from the alley.'

'Four men, four rifles, we'd be ripped apart anyway,' Ramés said.

'I'll take that chance,' Caroline Chauvin said, her face grim. 'I for one am not going quietly to jail.'

'You prefer getting yourself gunned down?'

Caroline's glance was withering.

'Action's better than a thousand wasted words,' she said, 'but I can see how that wouldn't appeal to a man with a mile-wide yellow streak.'

Face taut with anger, Ramés kneed his horse towards and made a grab for the dark-haired young woman.

He was too late. Caroline had executed a smooth cross draw. Pistol in hand, she spurred her horse up the alley. She rode straight towards the two men now cautiously walking their horses down towards the patch of waste ground. The two big bay geldings practically filled the alley's width. There was room for another horse to squeeze through – but only just, and it was risky: attempting it would take Caroline too close to the two men.

'Stupid cow,' Dom Ramés said breathlessly.

Again he urged his horse forward, but this time he was trying to save the young woman. The shotgun was in his hands. He lifted it, drove the butt into his shoulder. But he was unable to shoot. Caroline was between him and his targets. There was no chance of a clear shot. He relaxed his grip on the deadly weapon. Sitting straight in the saddle, he was held spellbound by the young woman's audacity.

Caroline Chauvin, a girl from New Orleans who was

33

completely out of her depth, had instinctively adopted shock tactics. Riding hard and fast at the two men, she closed the gap rapidly. A pistol cracked, again and again. She had begun firing. Her shots were not aimed. They were intended to add to the confusion. She fired rapidly, bent low over the horse's neck. Muzzle flashes painted the drab timber walls. Dark hair flying, she bore down on the two armed men.

'Go after her,' Boudreaux said. 'She's doing all the work but she needs help and three of you working together can force a way through.'

'Three?' Ramés said, flashing a glance at Boudreaux. 'I count four—'

'Someone has to stay here and hold off the others.'

'But you've got the money.'

'Forget the goddamn money, if we make it out of here we'll meet at the campsite—'

But now he was talking to their backs. Alice LaClaire had responded to his first order, and gone after Caroline. In her hand she held the six-gun she had used to threaten the bank manager and tucked somewhere under her skirts. Ramés had cast a last speculative glance in Boudreaux's direction then clamped his jaw shut and followed her. He rode precariously poised, gripping his mount with knees and thighs. Both hands were held high, clamped on the shotgun.

Watching them leave, Boudreaux eased his horse backwards. The open patch of rough waste ground was small. Two-storey buildings stood on the two short sides. The longer side running parallel to the alley was blocked by another run-down building with a shingle roof – but at that building's end there was a rickety paling fence. Some of those pales had fallen. Beyond, there was more open ground, clear daylight, bright sunshine.

The fierce crackle of gunfire snapped Boudreaux's head around. Ramés's shotgun boomed and there was the unmistakable sound of buckshot clattering into timber. One of the young women screamed. A man's deep voice began bellowing orders.

There was confusion on a grand scale. Into it rode the two men who had been guarding the town end of the alley. They spurred their horses up the slope. Their eyes were fixed as they looked straight ahead. They were riding towards the crackle of gunfire, the sound of excited voices, the desperate cries of injured men or women. Boudreaux had dropped right back. He held his horse hard up against a rotting timber wall, in deep shadow. Brandishing six-guns, the two men rode straight on by.

'Dammit, dammit, they're finished,' Boudreaux whispered, despair in the soft utterance as he pictured Ramés, Alice LaClaire and Caroline Chauvin facing two armed men and threatened by another two swiftly closing in from behind.

But if they were finished, Boudreaux reasoned, fiercely controlling his emotions, then it was his job to get clear. The bank robbery had gone badly wrong, but by standing back from the action he had created a situation that left him unobserved. No need for haste, no need to risk his horse by charging out of there like a madman.

The shooting had ceased, leaving an echoing sense of dullness in the ears, and gunsmoke was a sharp tang in his nostrils when he turned away from the alley. He could hear angry words being exchanged, fading as he rode across the waste ground. As he had hoped, his horse was able to pick up its hoofs and walk almost daintily straight through the paling fence and onto the patchy grass that lay beyond. From there it was a matter of working his way to the next cross street and riding the length of it and others until business premises and houses became fewer and more scattered as he came to the outskirts of town.

Five minutes later he was in open countryside and hot sunlight, riding unhurriedly in a northerly direction. He had left Coffeyville like a ghost. It would be a while before he was missed. He rode with a degree of contentment for, behind his saddle, the money was a solid, comforting weight in his saddle-bags. But uncertainty about the fate of his three comrades refused to go away; it remained with him, and was a nagging worry all the way back to the campsite they had left with such high hopes earlier that morning.

'We got one of them,' Marshal Dusty Miller said flatly. 'One got away.'

'Counting the two waiting in the alley, we got three,' said Tom Bellard, his dark-haired young deputy. 'Surely that's a good morning's work?'

'Not if the man who got away was the bank robber carrying the money.'

'Dammit. Is that right?'

They were in the Coffeyville marshal's office. Dom Ramés, Alice LaClaire and Caroline Chauvin had been locked up in separate cells. They had given their names freely, but when questioned about the man who had got away they refused to talk.

What they didn't know was that Miller had already identified Boudreaux from the stacks of Wanted dodgers in the office.

The young women's reluctance had nothing to do with some mythical code of the West, heroic self-sacrifice to protect a comrade: it was heartfelt loyalty, stubborn determination not to give up a comrade. Ramés had his own thoughts on the matter. The first was that Boudreaux was infamous, a killer, and that linking themselves to a man of his notoriety might ruin their chances of acquittal or a reduced sentence. Second thoughts brought another startling possibility, which he was secretly working on: could giving up a wanted criminal actually work in their favour?

Ramés finally said as much, raising his eyebrows as he awaited their response. It had come from Alice LaClaire. Her tongue lashing had brought a flush to Ramés's face.

Dom Ramés was nursing a gunshot wound in his left upper arm; it had been bandaged and strapped by the town doctor. LaClaire had a purple bruise on her cheekbone, Chauvin was unhurt, but both women had been badly shaken by the burst of violence that had been more frightening than dangerous. The shooting on both sides had been wild, hot lead punching holes in buildings or whining harmlessly into the blue skies. Alice LaClaire had been felled by a punch from one of the deputies when she tried to force her way through, Ramés shot by accident when he discharged his shotgun and fell from his horse into the path of a stray bullet. The fight had descended into farce. When the two deputies came charging in from the rear firing fierce volleys into the air, the battle was over, victory going almost by default to the upholders of the law.

Except for the missing money.

In the office, Miller had risen from his chair.

'I'll go talk to them again,' he said. 'Stick around, Tom. I've got a nasty feeling we're going to have our hands full with this trio, yet for the life of me I can't see why.'

A bull of a man, with a thick neck, massive shoulders and a shock of wiry grey hair, Miller had been appointed marshal of Coffeyville after the Daltons' failed raid on the Condon and first National banks. He had taken over from Marshal Connelly who, in attempting to stop the escaping Dalton boys, had rushed fearlessly into Death Alley and been shot in the back by Grat Dalton.

It was Miller who had vowed to stop any bank robbers who might attempt to etch their names in history alongside the Daltons and the James boys by going one better. Today he had been looking failure in the face and, though outwardly calm, he was in an ugly mood.

In the Coffeyville jail there were eight cells forming a square around a central space with a rough table and chairs. Three were occupied. The prisoners looked up when the door banged behind Miller as he came through from the office jingling his keys.

He went straight to Alice LaClaire's cell. She was reclining gracefully on the crude corn husk mattress, the navy-blue dress moulding itself to her slim form. Her usual self-confidence had returned as memories of the gunfight faded. She regarded Miller with a challenge in her blue eyes.

'Where did we go wrong?' she said as he entered her cell. 'You knew everything, didn't you – but how could that be?'

'I'm naturally suspicious, and I keep my eyes open,' Miller said. 'You were in town a week ago with that feller – what was his name again?'

He waited. She didn't answer the question by providing the information that would confirm something he was ninety per cent sure he already knew. Instead she grinned and shook her head.

'Go on. I was in town a week ago and. . . ?'

'You and that young feller were taking too much interest in the First National. You must have stood across the street, walked up and down looking at it and talking about it, for a good fifteen minutes. No bank's that interesting. I smelt a rat.'

'You mean you guessed what we were up to, and then you followed us?'

'Every inch of the way, even when you rode out of the plaza and up that alley between 8th and 9th Streets. You went through the same procedure there: looking, talking. I was puzzled. Why discuss a patch of waste ground? But I was not only puzzled, I was also intrigued. Something big was going on, and I couldn't wait to see what developed.'

'But in the end, that's what you had to do: after we rode out of town, it was all down to sitting and waiting.'

Miller nodded. He paced the cell, glanced across at the others, then back at Alice LaClaire.

'I must admit you would have fooled me and got away with it, you and that young feller rolling into town in a top-buggy, all dolled up in your Sunday best and pretty well unrecognizable as the pair I'd watched—'

'*Would* have fooled you?'

'That's right. You *stole* that clothing in town a week ago, the buggy just a couple of hours before you drove it into town. But I'd put word out a week ago, as soon as you left town – anything unusual happens, let me know, and fast. The buggy's owner did just that, and I guess you headed for town more sedately than he did when he rode in on his fastest horse to report the theft.'

'And the bank manager . . . Frank . . . was he following instructions and stringing us along?'

'As best he could. He's always a mite nervous, which is why I walked in to check how he was coping.'

'So . . . what now?' Alice looked across the open space to Caroline's cell and rolled her eyes. 'Will you listen to me? Asking "what now" is developing into a habit.'

'You'll say it on your wedding night,' Caroline said with a grin, 'if we ever get out of jail.'

'Oh, we will,' Alice said.

'It's just a question of when,' Miller agreed drily. 'I'd say confirming the name of your missing partner might help knock a few years off your sentence.'

'Don't hold your breath.'

'Well, that's no more than I expected. But while the offer's there, consider this: I don't know what arrangement you four had, but I can guess what your partner's thinking now. He's got five thousand dollars in his saddle-bags. He's free and running, and he'll be looking ahead, not back. Something tells me that if he thinks about you at all it'll be one night in a year's time when he's drinking his coffee by a camp-fire a thousand miles from here and finds himself wondering, without too much concern, what happened to you.'

Dom Ramés swore softly, and swung his legs around so that he was sitting on his cot. His face was pale. Blood had seeped through the bandage on his left arm. The white of the bandage contrasted sharply with his black attire.

'If I were you, Marshal, I'd be putting some thought to what you're going to do with us if we're convicted of attempted bank robbery.'

'There's no if, you *will* be convicted,' Miller said bluntly.

'A good lawyer could present an excellent case for the defence,' Ramés said. 'How about you considering this. Caroline and me, why, we were just two innocent bystanders. We'd ridden into Coffeyville, stopped a while to rest our horses on waste ground, and before we could catch our breath we were in the middle of a desperate shootout.'

'That's a load of bull,' Miller said, 'you're all in this together. You'll be convicted and you'll go to jail.'

'How?'

Miller frowned. 'What's that supposed to mean?'

'How do we go to jail? We can't serve time here. Kansas State penitentiary's in Lansing. We're talking two hundred miles or more north of Coffeyville. Now, I don't know if you're planning on using the railroad, or some kind of horse-drawn wagon to transport us that distance. But whatever you decide on, if we're convicted you'll have three desperate outlaws on your hands' – he grinned across at Alice – 'with others out there watching your every move. You know, I really don't fancy your chances of holding on to us all the way across the Kansas plains.'

41

'Are you saying there's more than one man out there? That you three and that feller who got away are members of an outlaw gang?'

Ramés shrugged.

'What I'm saying is you're like a man who's caught himself a spitting wild cat. He can't put it down because the damn thing'll rip him apart, yet he knows that wild cat's mate and the others in the pride are prowling in a tightening circle just waiting for an opportunity to pounce.'

FOUR

The deep, grassy basin on the Elk River where they had made their camp was thirty miles to the north-west of Coffeyville. Before setting off on the raid the four had conceded that things could go badly wrong. They would go ahead with the raid on the Coffeyville bank, but they had all agreed that, should they get involved in a gunfight, those who managed to get away and were still able to ride should make their way back to the hollow.

Taking his time, nursing his big bay through the sultry July heat, Jean Pierre Boudreaux arrived there a little before noon. He paused for a while on the lip of the hollow, washing out his mouth with brackish, lukewarm water from his canteen while he gazed in an absent way towards the empty campsite close to the glistening silver ribbon of the river. Despite the hot, dusty ride which should have settled his jangling nerves, his thoughts were still in turmoil. Unable to empty his mind, to put the Coffeyville disaster behind him, he spat out the water, grimaced, then started his horse down the twisting track through the mesquite.

Fifteen minutes later he had reached the trampled grass and the circle of stones enclosing the camp-fire's white ashes, removed the rig, the horse had drunk its fill and was nibbling at the lush grass close to the river and a fire was crackling under the coffee pot.

Close to the flames, sitting cross-legged with his saddle and the leather bag swollen with stolen money no more than ten feet away under the trees, Boudreaux closed his eyes and allowed the peace of the location to wash over him. He did it deliberately, willing his breathing, too fast still, to return to normal; willing his pulse, hissing in his ears and thumping uncomfortably in his chest, to settle and fade into the background.

He stayed there in repose for a good half-hour. Then, at last feeling as calm as he could reasonably expect in the circumstances, he splashed hot coffee into a tin cup, climbed to his feet and strolled down to the river. There, sipping the coffee, listening to the gentle hiss and lap of water on gravel, he stood and gazed in a brooding way towards the south; towards the unseen town of Coffeyville.

He'd come a long way. One morning six months ago he had woken in the dawn's early light, and by midday he was being hunted for the brutal murder of a man and woman in their eighties. An eyewitness had recognized him when he ran from the building, sick to the stomach after discovering the two bloody bodies. Newfangled technology had sealed his fate. There was no sense in turning himself in to the authorities to explain that he knew the old couple, that he had gone there to talk, to borrow money on the advice and recommendation of Caroline Chauvin, but never to steal, never to kill. He had always seen them alone, always at night. There were no witnesses to their friendship who could step forward to prove his innocence. He had been in the wrong place, at the wrong time. Chance had turned a good man into a fugitive. And now. . . ?

So, was this destiny? Was this what had drawn them to a lush hollow in southern Kansas, the quartet from New Orleans who had been drawn together by one man running away from a certain one-way trip to the gallows, and a thirst for adventure shared by all four of them?

Boudreaux and Alice LaClaire had been friends since childhood.

Caroline Chauvin was known to them. Although she had directed Boudreaux to the old couple, she had never expressed an opinion on his guilt or otherwise – which, he supposed, was understandable; if he had murdered the old couple after being sent there by Caroline, then she would be forced to blame herself for their deaths.

Dom Ramés was a casual acquaintance he hadn't seen for years. He had appeared out of nowhere, a man with a mysterious past hidden behind unreadable eyes who had asked to join the group. So they were two men and two young women who, over a period of more than six months, had ridden steadily north chasing an elusive dream that had never been clearly defined, never been put into words because not one of them could *find* the words.

Until recently. Until he read about the Daltons. But the dream that had been a glittering pot of gold at the end of a rainbow just over the horizon had turned into a nightmare and the only words Boudreaux could find now left him close to despair. For he was faced with a task more challenging than any bank robbery.

On that day when Boudreaux had returned from Wichita clutching yellowing newspapers and the four had gathered around the camp-fire to make their plans, they had reached an agreement: if the clever, daring bank robbery that was firing their imagination went badly wrong and one or more of them were caught and held, somehow those prisoners would be freed. Not before they were convicted, not before they were taken away to a state penitentiary, but before any trial.

No. Angrily, Boudreaux shook his head and started back up the river-bank. Oh, no, he thought, flinging himself down by the fire and dropping his head in his hands, their statement of intent at that increasingly sober gathering had been much more precise, much more demanding, because the dangers in what they were planning were clear. If they were caught and trapped when robbing the First National bank, if lawmen or members of the public were gunned down in an abortive attempt to escape, lynching was not a possibility – it was a probability. And so, they had agreed, every attempt should be made to free the prisoners *within hours of their arrest.*

But what they had never considered, Boudreaux thought bitterly, was the possibility that three of them could be taken and just one left to face that . . . that what? Impossible task?

Boudreaux lifted his head, and suddenly there was a thin smile on his face, a gleam in his dark, deep-set eyes.

No, nothing was impossible. If one man could dream of a way of doing something, *anything,* then another man

46

would turn up with a way of undoing it. A jail was nothing more than a building with walls and windows; a cell was just a room with bars, and a lock; a lawman was just a man – and man was a fallible beast.

Dom Ramés. Caroline Chauvin. And Alice.

For the first time, as a grotesque image appeared of Alice LaClaire, battered and despairing with torn clothes and her eyes red with weeping in the Coffeyville jail, a lump formed in Boudreaux's throat. He leaped to his feet, looked about him as if seeking the solution to all his problems in the parched trees, the placid river, the encircling mesquite slopes that hid them from the world and had drawn them to the hollow.

Then, drawing a deep breath, for the first time truly understanding that he *was* on his own, that no help was forthcoming, that it was down to him and nobody else to effect the escape of three prisoners from the Coffeyville jail, Jean Pierre Boudreaux began to pace restlessly as he turned his mind to the task that lay before him.

Seconds later he came to an abrupt halt as another thought struck him. He hadn't yet worked out what he was going to do, but one thing was certain: he would be returning to Coffeyville, and he could not take with him the one good thing to have come out of the bank raid. He had saddle-bags packed with stolen money. That, Boudreaux knew, would have to be hidden.

He spent the next five minutes carrying the bags with him as he looked for a suitable hiding place. A short way into the woods there was a fallen tree, with exposed roots. He pushed the saddle-bags into the hole left under the roots when the wind tore the tree out of the ground, and covered it with loose earth and dead leaves.

When he stepped back he was pleased with his handiwork. The saddle-bags were well hidden in earth that had been disturbed by a force of nature. The hollow on the Elk River was remote, and some distance from frequently used trails. If strangers happened upon it, the deserted campsite might intrigue them but the fallen tree was unlikely to attract their attention.

On the other hand, Boudreaux mused, if things again went badly wrong and he was gunned down in his attempt to rescue his friends but they made it back to the hollow, then it was important that they could find the cash; that it wasn't left there to rot.

After a moment's thought he used his foot to change the position of some of the rocks around the dead camp-fire. To a stranger, the arrangement would still look haphazard, and have no significance. To Ramés, Caroline and Alice, those rocks would now clearly be directing them to the fallen tree.

If, after that, they couldn't figure out what they were looking for, Boudreaux thought with a final look at his handiwork, then, goddammit, they surely didn't deserve the money.

FIVE

'That was fancy talking, Dom, you and those damn spitting wildcats,' Caroline Chauvin said, 'but I don't think you fooled Miller one bit. As far as he's concerned, he's got most of the bunch behind bars. Now it's a matter of getting us to trial.'

'Jean Pierre will make sure that doesn't happen,' Alice said.

'Jean Pierre,' Dom Ramés said, 'will have his work cut out.'

Well, yes, that could be right, Alice thought, not bothering to argue the point. Looked at coldly, she had to admit the task did seem impossible. On the other hand, she was a whole lot closer to Jean Pierre Boudreaux than Dom or Caroline. If any man could spring them from the Coffeyville jail, it was Jean Pierre.

It was mid afternoon. A little after midday a deputy had brought them a meal with plenty of strong coffee to wash it down, and after that they had dozed in their cells – or as best they could in stifling heat and on lumpy corn-husk mattresses. Now, gone three o'clock, they were all awake

49

and again sitting at the head of their iron cots. They were hugging their drawn-up knees, their backs were against hard stone walls. In Caroline's chilling words, they were getting a foretaste of the best they could expect from life for the next twenty years if they were convicted of armed robbery. And that was a certainty, she pointed out, if Marshal Dusty Miller was right about Jean Pierre.

'Oh, he'll have his work cut out all right,' she said now, 'but that's only if he makes the attempt. Miller painted an ugly picture, but a man out there with five thousand dollars in his saddle-bags is going to be sorely tempted to keep on riding.'

Alice gave an unladylike snort.

'That's insulting, and you know it. Jean Pierre will come good. He'll get us out of here. What I can't figure out is how, or when.'

'Whatever he's got planned, he'll do it at night,' Ramés said.

Caroline pulled a face. 'That's what they'll expect. They'll be waiting for him.'

'He'll create a diversion.'

'One man can't do that. To create a diversion you need a partner playing the part of a drunken cowboy shooting up another part of the town, breaking windows, starting a saloon brawl – something like that.'

'A clever man will find other ways of doing it,' Alice said.

'Name one,' Ramés said.

Again she snorted. 'It's not me out there, it's Jean Pierre. Have a little faith, Dom. We don't need to know how, all we need to know is Jean Pierre's out there trying

– and he'll do it, I *know* he will.'

'He'd better,' Ramés said. 'Because if he can't do it, we'll have to rely on the good Lord to get us out of here.'

The nervousness he had been keeping under tight control suddenly seemed to break though. He had been touching his bandages, plucking at the rawhide cord he wore around his neck, scratching his dark hair and drawing glances of scarcely veiled contempt from Caroline. Now he swung his legs off the cot, stepped down onto the hard floor and began pacing restlessly.

Alice noticed his sudden lack of control, and smiled in a superior way.

'I have faith in flesh and blood, Dom. A man walking upright on two legs, with a pistol clenched in his big fist.'

For a few moments they sat in silence. Despite the optimism in her words, deep inside Alice was feeling much less sanguine. Jean Pierre was on his own, and they were locked in barred cells in a stone building in the centre of Coffeyville. To free them, Jean Pierre had to get in, then they had to get out. One way in and out was through the office, and that was guarded by armed lawmen. If they made it as far as the street, they would need horses, and Miller would make damn sure there were no horses tied at the rail. Jean Pierre could ride into town in the middle of the night without any trouble, but no man for whom stealth is a necessity could approach the jail without being noticed if three horses were trotting behind him at the end of a rope.

There was a back door, between the cells – but it was bolted, and looked unused.

In the dead of night, he could break in through the

51

roof, Alice thought, brightening. He could bring ropes. We could all climb out. Even town marshals have to sleep.

'If he came from the back of the jail he could always tie a rope to the bars on the window and use a horse to pull them out,' Caroline said, breaking the silence. 'Isn't that what they do?'

'That, or use sticks of dynamite to knock that back door off its hinges or blow the walls down,' Ramés said, grinning – and then he raised a cautioning finger to his lips as the door leading to the office banged open and Miller came through. The deputy was behind him. He remained in the doorway, his hand on the butt of his six-gun.

'What was that about dynamite?' the marshal said, approaching Ramés's cell with his keys jingling.

'We're thinking of going into the mining business when we get out of here,' Ramés said.

'Consider yourself part of the way there,' Miller said, and he used one of the keys to open Ramés's cell.

'You mean we're getting out now?'

'Out of here, for your own safety. What the Dalton boys did to the town raised hackles. A lot of hard men are still angry. I've heard rumours of a lynching, and it's pretty clear you stand little chance of a fair trial. So, you're being moved to Topeka. You'll be safe in the state capital, and that's where you'll be tried.'

He had been busy while talking, and by the time he'd run out of words all three prisoners were out of the cells and standing in the open area under the watchful eyes of the deputy, Tom Bellard. They were shepherded through to the office. Several men in suits were waiting there. The room was crowded, and Alice watched nervously as papers were shuffled, documents signed.

When they were ushered out onto the sunlit plank walk a tall man with a dove-grey Stetson, elegant jacket swept back from a gleaming Colt Peacemaker and matching pants tucked into shiny boots was standing by an old, shabby Concord stagecoach. His manner was bored, his face expressionless. Through the open jacket a badge could be seen pinned to a fancy brocade vest.

'Federal Marshal Jake Hustler,' Miller said, by way of introduction. 'He'll be your escort—'

'Guard,' Ramés said.

Miller glared. 'The coach has been brought out of retirement. The driver up there on the box will get you to Topeka, with stops for refreshment along the way. If you cause trouble—'

'We won't,' Alice said. 'We'd rather be safe in a Topeka jail than facing a lynching here in Coffeyville.'

She said the words partly because she knew that was what Miller would expect, but also because her mind was racing. She was recalling Ramés's earlier words. *I don't know if you're planning on using the railroad, he'd said, or some kind of horse-drawn wagon to transport us that distance. But whatever you decide on you'll have three desperate outlaws on your hands.*

What he might have added, Alice thought, as she exchanged glances with Ramés and Caroline and tried to signal her excitement to them while fighting to calm her racing pulse, was that in a coach those three desperate outlaws would be one thin panel of wood away from freedom. Now, to their obvious and utter disbelief, that was what had come to pass. Guarded by one man, they were being taken from the confines of secure jail cells and driven in a dilapidated Concord coach out onto the open Kansas plains. They would never, ever, have a better chance of making the break for freedom.

But where, she thought, as the driver called to his team and the coach jerked into motion, did their unexpected departure leave Jean Pierre Boudreaux?

SIX

It was oppressively dark when Boudreaux rode into Coffeyville after midnight. The night was moonless. Thick cloud had drifted in from the west. It formed a blanket, trapping the heat of the day, causing the sweat to spring out on a man's skin. Boudreaux rode with extreme caution, entering the town like a man passing through the door into the lion's den. He knew that the lawman with the strength of a bull in his thick frame would have retained in his mind an image of the young man in the suit who had leaped down from the top-buggy and proceeded to rob the bank, and Boudreaux had work to do within spitting distance of the jail.

Indeed, he thought, his face set and grim in the darkness, his work would take him all the way *into* the jail – but not before he had carried out certain tasks, prepared the ground for an escape that must not fail.

He rode almost all the way to the plaza, then turned away from the main streets and slipped almost silently into the top end of the alley between 8th and 9th streets. He rode a further fifty yards, and ground-tethered his horse on the patch of waste ground that was becoming familiar. Tempting fate? Possibly. But for what he was about to do he needed space, and a location Caroline, Alice and Dom Ramés could run to without a second thought when they came bursting out of the jail.

Satisfied, Boudreaux walked cautiously down to the plaza end of the alley.

There was no sign of life. Standing in deep shadow tight up against the side of one of the buildings, wary, vigilant, he cast his mind back to that first visit to Coffeyville when he and Alice had familiarized themselves with the town. They had concentrated on the area around the bank, and on planning an escape route, but they had also looked beyond the plaza and the streets in the immediate vicinity. Boudreaux needed a general store. He needed a livery barn. It took but a moment's thought to recall the location of both those establishments.

He'd already worked out the order in which various tasks must be carried out. The livery barn was where he would begin – and that first call was also the moment when Boudreaux's plans moved from clever ideas to dangerous reality. It was a time, he figured, for girding his loins, and it was with a giddy feeling of standing outside himself and watching his actions from afar that Boudreaux slipped along the shadowy plank walks of Coffeyville and so came to the livery barn.

The double doors were open. No lights were showing. Boudreaux stepped inside. He pulled one of the doors shut, grimacing as the old timber scraped noisily across uneven earth and sharp stones. When he turned towards the interior he could feel on his face the moist warmth from horses in the stalls, could smell them and hear their breathing and sudden restless movements as they in turn caught his scent. As his eyes grew accustomed to the gloom he became aware of the sheen of worn leather, the glitter of metal. He needed three horses, three rigs. Nothing to it. Take any three rigs, saddle three good horses and lead them back to the waste ground.

Boudreaux took a deep breath, and set to work. He had led the horses from the stalls and had saddled the second horse and was down tightening the cinch when the white-haired hostler came stumbling out of his sleeping quarters dressed in grubby long underwear, yawning his head off and carrying a badly dented, smoking oil lamp and a sawn-off shotgun.

Damn it.

'I needed my horse in a hurry,' Boudreaux called quickly, moving without menace towards the old man. 'This time of night, disturbing you seemed an unnecessary intrusion. I was going to leave the money I owe you where you would see it—'

'I ain't seen *you* before, mister,' the hostler said in a gravelly voice, 'and that's two horses you've got saddled, another one waitin'.'

'My horses, which is exactly what I told you,' Boudreaux said smoothly. 'I should have realized you've just woken up, and spoken slowly to make myself clear. Anyway, now we've got that straightened out. . . .'

While holding the hostler's attention by talking total nonsense, he had moved in close. The lamp was held high, casting its wan light on Boudreaux's face. The shotgun was pointing at the ground. The old man was staring right through Boudreaux with rheumy eyes that were unfocused as he searched a confused memory.

In one swift movement, Boudreaux drew his six-gun and slammed the barrel across the side of the hostler's head. The crack was like a blacksmith's hammer striking stone. The old man grunted and went down in a pathetically small grey heap. Boudreaux caught the shotgun before it could hit the ground and discharge. The lamp landed in the thin layer of straw covering the hard-packed earth runway. The glass cracked. The wick continued to burn. Oil seeped out in a spreading black stain.

For an instant Boudreaux looked at it, lips pursed as his mind registered the possibilities. Then he walked away from the unconscious old man and quickly finished saddling the three horses.

Before he led them out into the street, he dropped to one knee by the old man and felt his pulse. He was alive. A trickle of blood in his grey hair was the only sign that he wasn't in a deep sleep. Boudreaux stood up, held the hostler under both arms and dragged him out through a back door. He left him curled up against a wall on the far side of the rear alley.

Then he went back inside and deliberately kicked the shattered oil lamp further into the livery barn. It bounced, trailing oil, thumped hard against one of the stalls and came to rest in dry straw that had gathered in the angle between the ground and the thin timber wall.

The flame continued to burn.

Outside, the street was still deserted. However, the hostler's surprise interruption had served warning on

Boudreaux that he was riding his luck. Aided by a growing familiarity with the town's layout, he was able to lead the horses into a side street and make his way back to the waste ground where he had left his horse, using narrow alleyways and seldom-used thoroughfares.

The patch of open ground was an area of comparative lightness in the dark night. Swiftly Boudreaux loose-tethered the stolen horses to the unbroken section of the paling fence. Then he mounted his own horse, made his way to the plaza and rode down main street. That ride took him past the jail. There was a light in the window, and he thought he could see movement. His skin prickling, Boudreaux rode by. When he had almost reached the general store, he pulled his horse into the shadows and sat allowing his nerves to calm as he marshalled his thoughts.

The store was on the opposite side of the street from the livery barn, on the same side of the street as the jail. Next to the livery barn there was a two-storey hotel. When they had made their first visit to Coffeyville, Boudreaux and Alice had split up for a time and Alice had made her own discreet enquiries. She had learned that Marshal Dusty Miller was a single man who lived in a room on the top floor of that hotel.

The hotel and the livery barn could be seen from the jail.

Tonight, Boudreaux was assuming that Miller had gone to bed, leaving the jail in charge of the deputy who was on night shift. That put Miller in the hotel, the deputy in the jail, Ramés, Caroline Chauvin and Alice LaClaire locked in their respective cells.

The scene was set.

Boudreaux lifted his head, and sniffed. Then he cast a searching glance across the street. One of the livery barn's doors was closed, as he had left it. The other was open. Boudreaux could smell wood smoke, the faint reek of burning coal oil. He could also, he thought, see a light flickering inside the barn – and it was growing brighter.

He looked at the gap between the barn and the hotel. It was narrow. There was no alley, just a space between two walls, littered with rubbish. If he could trust his senses, the broken oil lamp he had kicked had ignited the straw in the barn and the flames were already licking up the timber walls of the stall. If he waited long enough it was possible that the fire would quickly spread to the adjoining building.

Possible. But not certain.

Irritably, Boudreaux shook his head. He couldn't risk leaving anything to chance. His plans were incomplete. With the decision made, he slipped from his horse and walked quickly to the front of the general store. In all probability the owner lived above the shop. Well, the best Boudreaux could hope for was that the man and his wife were heavy sleepers. He stepped up to the store's door, tried the handle – and bared his teeth when the door refused to open. He took a deep breath, stepped back, then hit the door hard with his shoulder.

It burst open. There was the sound of wood splintering. Boudreaux grabbed the door before it could crash against whatever lay inside. Then he stepped into the dark interior, pushed the door to and stood listening.

Upstairs, a man was coughing. The coughing subsided, ceased. Boudreaux waited in the silence. It dragged on.

No boards creaked overhead. Nobody called out, demanding to know who was there.

Boudreaux counted to sixty. His eyes gradually adjusted to the gloom. Too soon, he began searching the shop. A pile of assorted goods went clattering to the board floor when he stumbled against it. He held his breath, his eyes squeezed shut. Did some more counting. Then he was off again, a blind man with arms outstretched, eyes at last adjusting, picking out shapes that in the darkness were distorted and menacing. Sweating, heart thumping, ears aching with the strain of listening, he found what he was looking for mainly by touch and smell. The coal oil was in one gallon rectangular cans. He took one, then continued his search until he found a bolt of material. He tried to tear off a strip. The cotton was too strong. More time passed as he took out his pocket knife and used the big blade to nick the edge of the cloth. This time the material ripped easily. Carrying his finds, carefully avoiding the clutter and the goods he had knocked over, he went to the door and slipped out into the night.

In the shadow of the shop's covered gallery he unscrewed the can's cap, twisted the strip of material, then poked most of its length into the can and held it there until it was soaked in coal oil. Then he pulled the makeshift wick part way out and left it hanging.

Boudreaux stood back. He looked across the street. The interior of barn was now brightly lit by the flames. Smoke was leaking out through the open door and flattening against the front of the building as it streamed up towards the night sky.

Another quick glance up the street told him that the

fire had not yet been noticed by the men in Dusty Miller's office. He had time, but the fire was spreading quickly and the smell of smoke was strong. Hesitation was getting him nowhere; if the blaze in the barn burst through the roof or the side walls, the alarm would certainly be raised and he could be caught out in the open by the deputy when he came running from the jail, a man carrying a can of coal oil within yards of a raging fire.

For the first time Boudreaux admitted that he was about to commit an appalling crime. Already responsible for a fire that could reach and burn to death an unconscious old hostler, he was now about to throw a can of burning oil into an occupied hotel. His intention was to create a diversion, trusting that the town's marshal would be awake to the danger, and be fit enough to escape. But there were almost certainly other guests, some young, some old, and he was about to put their lives in immediate danger so that he could set free three prisoners who would, at worst, be convicted of armed robbery.

For several long minutes, with the crackle and roar of the livery barn fire increasing and the acrid smell of smoke so strong that his eyes were beginning to water, Jean Pierre Boudreaux hesitated.

Then, face set, teeth gritted, he took a firm grip on the can of oil, stepped down off the plank walk and started across the street.

SEVEN

'I can't believe they let him slip through their fingers,' Jim Gatlin said.

'There's worse,' Charlie Pine said. 'That feller who got away with all that money, we can't even be sure it was Boudreaux. It's true Miller sighted him in town a couple of weeks ago, and he made a point of walking in when the feller was sitting ice-cool in the bank manager's office. But the man had changed his clothes, looked a different person, and Miller's beginning to have doubts. Also, the young woman who robbed the bank with Boudreaux – if it was him – refused point blank to give Miller his name.'

'And now the three they caught are on their way to Topeka.'

'Yes. Imprisonment, then trial. Out of our reach.'

'Technically, they're not.' Gatlin said. 'They're withholding information about a man wanted for murder, Charlie. As Pinkerton agents we have the right to visit and question.'

'Yes, I know that. But if we go down that road we're looking at formal applications, maybe wires passed back and forth between McParland up in Denver and authorities in Topeka to verify our identities and official status – and all that takes time.'

'OK, so assuming it was Boudreaux,' Gatlin said, 'where do you suppose he is now?'

Pine grimaced. 'Put yourself in his place. With a saddle-bag stuffed with greenbacks, I'd be long gone. Forget this talk of honour among thieves. Boudreaux can afford to disappear. Maybe he'll keep an eye on the newspapers, feel a twinge of remorse when his partners are sent to the pen up there in Lansing. That'll soon pass. You ask me, we won't hear of him again until he runs short of cash.'

'That's not Marshal Miller's opinion. He's convinced Boudreaux will be back.'

'Right. And like a good lawman, he's done something about it. I hope it works out for him. I think what he's doing is risky.'

It was close to one o'clock in the morning. The two Pinkerton agents were in Gatlin's hotel room across from the Coffeyville jail.

Gatlin was tall, lean, as dark as an Indian but with startlingly blue eyes. They could be as warm as summer skies, as cold as ice, but never deceptive: men who crossed Jim Gatlin's path always knew exactly where they stood.

Charlie Pine was of medium height, muscular, and behind his brown eyes there was always a hint of laughter. This was a dangerous characteristic: some very tough men had decided he was laughing at them, and acted accordingly. The fact that Pine was still alive and healthy was testimony to his strength, and his expertise with a gun.

Gatlin and Pine had been talking for more than an

hour, mostly about the audacious and imaginative plan to rob Coffeyville's First National Bank. Five thousand dollars had been taken, so in that respect the robbery had succeeded. As far as Gatlin and Pine were concerned, the missing cash was a minor consideration. They'd made the long train journey south-east from Denver with the sole aim of apprehending the New Orleans killer, Jean Pierre Boudreaux.

'If you're right about Boudreaux,' Jim Gatlin said, 'we're wasting time anyway and the only sensible thing to do is get a good night's sleep and head back to Denver.'

'Looks like it. When the prisoners were in Miller's jail it made sense to hang on in the hope Boudreaux would try to get 'em out. But they're not. If he is going to do something, it has to be on the trail between here and Topeka. You could make a case for us travelling with that coach, in the hope that Boudreaux would appear. We didn't do that, and I'd say it's now too late.'

'So. . . ?'

Pine grinned. 'So you're right. There's work for us, but it's in Denver, not Coffeyville or some desolate place out there on the baking Kansas plains.'

'Chasing a coach that's already got a federal marshal on board who should be able to handle anything Boudreaux can throw at him.'

'Unless Boudreaux's not on his own, in which case Marshal Jake Hustler could be in trouble.'

Gatlin merely grunted. For several minutes he had been aware of a faint smell of burning. That smell was becoming almost strong enough to bring tears to the eyes and, with a quick glance at Pine, he strode over to the window and pulled back the curtains.

Pine stood up, and quickly buckled on his gun-belt.

'Anything?'

Gatlin nodded. 'There's a lot of light flickering on the buildings opposite. Something's on fire, on this side of the street. If it's not us, it's the livery barn.'

He'd let the curtains fall back and was by the bed grabbing his gun-belt as he spoke. Both men headed for the door. Pine dragged it open and they pounded along the landing and started down the stairs.

As they did so there was the sound of a door banging open. Cool night air washed over their faces. Then something heavy landed in the downstairs reception area. There was the soft whoomp of an explosion. Suddenly the stairway was awash with light, and black smoke billowed upwards in a choking cloud.

The sudden blast of brilliant light and intense heat as the coal oil ignited drove Boudreaux back off the step and onto the plank walk. He could smell his eyebrows singeing. Black blotches danced before his eyes. The smoke caught at the back of his throat. He coughed and turned away. Through watering eyes he saw that the fire in the livery barn had not yet taken hold on the timber walls; had not yet attracted attention.

All that would change, and very quickly. Two fires would not go unnoticed. The occupants of the hotel would raise the alarm. From now on the time available to him was leaking away as fast as water from a bullet-riddled water tank.

As he crossed the street with his home-made bomb, he

had been undecided. Window, or door? He had opted for the hotel's front door, and tossed the can of oil with its burning fuse into the dark hallway as a calculated delaying tactic. Fire at the front of the building would drive Miller away, force him to seek a back door – if the marshal managed to get down the stairs. The thought that the man could be trapped with no way out brought a fleeting feeling of panic, of disgust at what he had done. Then he banished the weakening thoughts, leaped down into the street and ran towards the jail.

As he mounted the opposite plank walk he heard a sudden commotion behind him. Hand on the jail's door, he snatched a backward glance. A man had come tumbling out of the hotel, hands flapping at his clothes. He was followed by a second man who called something unintelligible as he lifted a hand and pointed towards Boudreaux.

Snarling with frustration, Boudreaux drew his six-gun. Then, taking a deep breath, he pushed open the door and stepped quickly into the jail.

The office was empty. A single oil lamp burned on the desk. Frowning, Boudreaux crossed the small room to an inner door. He opened it and stepped through. He was in the cell block. It was strangely silent – though he thought he could detect the faint sound of someone breathing.

Boudreaux closed the door behind him. Weak light from the office's single oil lamp, seeping under the door, reached a central open space, a table, and revealed the vague outline of the surrounding cells. That feeble light faded to nothing before it reached those barred rooms. In the nearest of them Boudreaux thought he could just make out a figure stretched full length under a rumpled blanket. The blanket was pulled all the way up over the sleeper's face. At the foot of the iron cot, medium-sized dusty boots stuck out from the blanket, the toes pointing to the roof.

Dom Ramés – or one of the girls?

Ears alert to any sounds from behind him, Boudreaux walked softly across the open area and tried the cell door. It was unlocked. His skin prickled. What the hell was going on? Hesitating, he used up precious seconds looking about him. He was now much closer to all the cells. His eyes began adjusting to the faint light. He stared into each barred room in turn, trying to penetrate the gloom. They were all, he decided, unoccupied.

Deep inside his head, alarm bells began to ring. Instinct was screaming at him to turn and run; his stubborn streak was urging him into the cell. Curiosity killed the cat, he remembered – but the inquisitive animal probably died happy. He smiled coldly, then pushed open the cell door and strode quickly to the bunk. With his left hand he grasped the edge of the blanket. He held his six-gun high, ready to strike. With one sharp flick of the wrist he stripped the single thin blanket from the inert figure.

Involuntarily, he took a shocked step backwards.

Marshal Dusty Miller was lying flat. One hand was by his side. The other rested on his belly. It was holding a six-gun. As the blanket was jerked away he emitted a startled grunt. His eyes flicked open. Boudreaux met the marshal's blank gaze. He saw the bleariness of sleep; incomprehension; sudden startled awareness followed by recognition. Then the eyes narrowed, the lips tightened.

For those rapidly changing shades of emotion to flicker across Miller's face it took mere fractions of a second. But the final tightening of his lips, the narrowing of the eyes, told Boudreaux that the man had come to his senses and was about to explode into action.

With a grunt, he brought the six-gun sweeping down in a wide arc and struck the marshal a vicious blow on the side of the head. The crack of metal striking bone was sickeningly loud in the silence. The gun twisted in Boudreaux's hand. The barrel's foresight split Miller's scalp. His head rocked. Blood flowed swiftly, darkly staining his wiry grey hair. The open eyes flickered, rolled back into his head. There was a gurgling deep in his throat. His eyes closed to slits and he began breathing stertorously through his open mouth.

The fingers holding the six-gun relaxed, opened. The pistol slid from his body to the mattress. Boudreaux picked it up and thrust into his belt. Again he gripped the blanket. This time he dragged it up, covering the unconscious man from head to toe. Then he spun on his heel and walked out of the cell.

He stood looking at the cells, a frown on his face. They were empty – so where were the prisoners? Wherever they were, Miller had obviously been expecting Boudreaux to return to Coffeyville. He had been lying in wait, but had fallen asleep and had paid—

A sudden sound from the office brought Boudreaux spinning around. Heart pounding, he stood listening. He heard a door bang. There was a dull metallic sound that could have been the working of a rifle's oiled action. Sharp words were exchanged between unseen men. They were followed by an ominous silence.

Boudreaux looked around the cell block. He was standing like a startled fox, stock still by the table in the open space. He saw now that in that surrounding square composed of eight unoccupied cells there was an opening. It led between the sides of two of the cells to the building's back wall. In that wall, there was a door.

Boudreaux ran to it.

It was bolted on the inside.

Cursing, he grabbed the iron bolt and tried to draw it, but the metal parts were held immovable by a combination of rust and years of dirt.

The seconds were ticking away. Boudreaux flashed a desperate look behind him. He looked up at barred windows; at a roof that was out of reach. Inevitably, drawn by a deathly silence that was more unnerving than a direct and violent attack, he looked at the door leading to the office.

He had no doubt that the voices he had heard belonged to the two men who had escaped from the fire he started in the hotel. That they were holding back could be for one reason only: they were unsure of what lay on this side of the door. In truth, from this position Boudreaux knew he could hold off any number of men for an indefinite period – but what good would it do him? There would be a Mexican stand-off. He could continue to shoot anyone who tried to come through the door until his ammunition ran out. But when it did there would certainly be dead bodies, he might be unscathed, but he would still be a prisoner in the cell block.

A prolonged siege of any kind would not help Dom

Ramés, Caroline Chauvin or Alice LaClaire. If they had been moved, they were still prisoners facing trial. If they had escaped. . . .

Boudreaux had not, until now, considered that possibility. The thought was so outrageous that he at once saw the funny side. He chuckled softly, holding back hysterical laughter, his shoulders shaking as he imagined the secure hollow in the hills, his partners rolled up in their blankets as they slept by the glowing embers of the camp-fire.

The door leading to the office began to open. It opened outwards. The movement was slow, inexorable. From being a narrow sliver of yellow light from the oil lamp the gap between door and post began to widen. Suddenly Boudreaux could see Caroline's gun-belt on the office's wall pegs; then the half-open street door; then part of the window.

Watching from the gloom, he realized that the door had stopped moving.

In complete silence, dry-mouthed, Jean Pierre Boudreaux sank to one knee and levelled his six-gun at the door.

EIGHT

The coach pulled into Wilson's station a little before ten o'clock. The building was low-slung, built of logs, with several open windows along its length. It had a stable at one end; alongside that, a corral that had once been used for spare stage teams but now held just three ragged, saddled ponies. To the rear a fence encircled a patch of stubbled growth. Beyond that the sun was a golden memory behind distant western hills, its light already paled to insignificance by the rising crescent moon.

The building's heyday had been in the glory days of the overland stagecoaches. The arrival of the railroad had driven most of the coach companies out of business. Wilson's station was now a run-down hostelry catering to drifters, travelling drummers, cowboys who wandered in from time to time from the scattering of ranches that were too far from small towns such as Elk City, Buffalo and Howard.

Marshal Jake Hustler stood well back as Dom Ramés, Caroline and Alice stepped stiffly down from the coach. His Peacemaker was in his hand. He had positioned himself so that if the prisoners made a break there was nowhere they could run that was not inside the arc he had covered.

The lanky coach driver climbed down from the boot, carrying his shotgun. He too stood clear of the three bank robbers. With Ramés leading the way they walked towards the low building and through the open door into the stink of coal oil, stale fried food, alcohol and cigarette smoke. There was another rank smell that Alice quickly realized came from the part-cured animal skins hanging on the log walls. That stink, she guessed, was the reason for the open windows.

Hustler followed them in. The driver had drifted away to tend to his team. Seated at a long pine table set centrally under smoking oil lamps, three unshaven men in rough clothing and carrying an assortment of deadly weapons paused in their game of stud poker and watched and listened without change of expression as Hustler stood at the black-painted bar and ordered four meals from the bearded and begrimed Joel Wilson. The order given, the marshal turned to face the room.

'I'm a United States federal marshal,' he said, his eyes fixed on the poker players. 'The three people I've brought in here tried to rob the bank at Coffeyville. Second time in less than a year that's happened, second time it's failed.' He cast a glance in Alice's direction at those words, as if challenging her to argue. 'If they make a break for it,' he went on, 'I expect every man here to come to the assistance of the law.'

And that, Alice thought, is unlikely to happen. She was still dressed in the long navy-blue dress that had once been elegant but now looked like something she had sewn together from remnants. But above it her shining blonde hair had already attracted the attention of the poker players. They had stared at her, she had looked back boldly and had weighed them up shrewdly in that one long glance: they were ruffians, renegades; they would treat any law officer with contempt, any lady with respect.

To eat their meal of fried beef and eggs the prisoners sat at the other end of the long table from the poker players. Hustler remained at the bar, drinking, smoking and eating as he talked to Wilson and the coach driver. He was between the prisoners and the door. As far as Alice could tell, there was no other way out.

Ramés was watching her, absently pulling at the cord around his neck. As if reading her thoughts he grimaced and waggled his head from side to side, expressing doubt.

'We have to try,' Alice said, leaning forward and talking softly. 'Now we're out of the coach we've got our feet on the ground. There's three saddled horses in the corral. If we use some God-given ingenuity, it should be possible.'

'The saddled horses belong to those characters playing poker. Steal them, we might as well cut our own throats. But that's supposing we could get out there in the first place – which we can't.'

'There is one way,' Caroline Chauvin said. 'It involves sacrifice, some acting ability, and the ability to flutter eyelashes.'

Alice frowned, her mind racing.

'The only way out is through the front door,' she said. 'If you're suggesting one of us engages Hustler in deep conversation while the other two make a run for it, it won't work. They've still got to get past him and that damn coach driver with his shotgun.'

'Why not make use of the open window at this end of the room?' Caroline said.

'Jesus!' Ramés breathed. 'It's in full view, that's why, and to get out fast enough we'd have to go head first.'

'Don't worry, you won't break any bones, there's nothing out there but dust. The window's ten yards from the corral. Take two of the saddled horses, cut the other's cinch. Hustler'll be left with the coach, or a scrawny nag that needs saddling. So you'll be gone, spurring those horses into the distance, and Hustler will be able to do nothing but fret and fume while he watches your dust.'

There was silence for a few moments. Alice was still eating. Ramés had finished. He was watching Caroline with a pensive look on his thin face.

'The way you're putting it, the words you're using,' he said at last, 'it sounds as if you've already decided I'm one of those making the break. If that's right, who's the other?'

'Alice.'

'Why?'

'Because she's always been close to Jean Pierre.'

'Maybe, but I think you're wrong. That dress will slow her down.'

'And she might spoil your chances?'

'Yes, all right, that's true.' Ramés scowled. 'But there's another reason. In here that outfit and her blonde hair has already got every man in the room looking at her. They'll do the same when she walks over to talk to Hustler. You're dressed for riding, you should come with me.'

She smiled sweetly. 'I don't like you, and I wouldn't

trust you as far as I can throw you.'

'So why send Alice out with a man like me?'

'Because I'm tougher than Alice.'

'Don't you be fooled by my fragile beauty,' Alice said.

'Fair enough, but I'm also a loner. I can look after myself. There's nothing Hustler can do to me but take me on to Topeka. Or try to.' She smiled. 'Nobody thought to search us when we were locked up; they just took the weapons they could see. But there's one Miller didn't see, and that's what's going to get me away from Hustler.'

'The little Remington over-and-under you've got tucked in your boot,' Alice said.

Her attention had shifted, and she was looking towards the bar. Wilson was nowhere to be seen. Hustler and the coach driver were still talking, still drinking, both men looking flushed. The poker players had been getting noisier, and Alice knew that was down to the quantity of alcohol they'd been pouring down their throats. If she and Ramés made the break now, Hustler's reactions would be impaired, the coach driver likely to shoot himself in the foot. She was certain the poker players would side with the escaping prisoners. In their present condition, they could get away with it, blaming their clumsiness as they got in Hustler's way on the whiskey they'd consumed.

'Saved by a bunch of drunks,' she said softly.

Caroline caught on at once, and was amused.

'Do it now,' she said. 'Leave it any longer, those men won't be able to stand and we need them between Hustler, you and that window.'

'You first. Get over there and flutter your eyelashes at that cocky marshal. He'll go weak at the knees.'

Under cover of the table she began tucking up her dress as Caroline made her way to bar. At once, Alice knew it was going to work. All eyes followed the dark-haired woman in the fringed leather pants and Confederate shirt as she walked down the room. When she reached Hustler she moved in close; when he tried to back off, she placed a hand on his shoulder and said something that brought a grin to his face. Adroitly, she manoeuvred him so that his back was to Alice and Ramés. The coach driver had also turned that way. The charade was being watched intently by the poker players, and Wilson was still out of the room.

'Let's go,' Alice said.

Moving with stealth and speed she and Ramés rose, left the table and made for the nearest window. Ramés went first. He hesitated for an instant, and Alice knew he was looking for an easy way out. There was none, and in any case they had no time. He stepped forward, then awkwardly tumbled head first through the opening. He landed on his hands, tucked in his head, rolled and regained his feet.

Alice grimaced. Could she do that? A quick sideways glance told her that all attention was still focused on the bar. Hustler and the coach driver had their backs turned. Caroline was talking earnestly, but Alice knew that over the lawman's shoulders her friend could see down the length of the room and knew what was going on.

Caroline will be urging me on, she thought. She'll be willing me to get on with it, to go before she runs out of talk and it's too late.

Alice took a deep breath, and threw herself out of the window.

She landed on her hands, tried to execute a forward roll. Her arms gave way. Her face hit the ground and she took in a mouthful of dust as she fell sideways and finished up in an ungainly sprawl. The tucked-up long dress had been pushed higher, exposing her long white legs. At the end of them her brown ankle boots looked like something worn by a circus clown.

Spitting, scrambling to her feet, she saw that Ramés was bent double, hands on knees. When he straightened up she realized he was almost helpless with laughter.

'Get moving, you damn fool,' she said angrily.

Rushing past him with one hand clutching her dress's long skirt, she swung a punch at his shoulder. She ran past the empty stable to the corral, slipped the loop of rope up over the post and pushed open the gate. The horses seemed too tired or too old to move. She ran to the one she judged to be the fastest, hoisted her skirt high, grabbed the horn and swung into the saddle.

Ramés was about to mount one of the two remaining saddled horses.

'Use your knife,' Alice yelled, throwing caution to the winds. 'Cut that one's cinch, dump the rig, take the other and let's get out of here.'

Quickly he dragged a bone-handled knife from his boot and ran to the remaining horse, a gaunt black figure with a naked blade flashing in the moonlight. He placed a steadying hand on the saddle, and bent down.

Kneeing her horse towards the open gate, casting apprehensive looks back towards the main building, Alice heard the snick as leather parted, the thud as Ramés dragged the saddle to the ground, the pound of boots as he ran back to the other horse.

She looked back. He had mounted, and was turning the horse to follow her. Unbelievably, he was again helpless with laughter. He was bent over in the saddle. One hand was raised. His finger was pointing at her naked legs. In the moonlight she could see tears of laughter glistening on his cheeks.

Then Wilson appeared. He emerged from the shadows at the rear of the station. He lifted a shotgun, levelled it, pulled both triggers. The explosion was like a bomb going off. The muzzle flash lit up the log walls.

Dom Ramés was still looking at Alice and laughing when the immense double charge of buckshot whined through the air above his head. He froze in mid-grin. For an instant it looked as if he might fall from the horse.

Then Alice saw common sense kick in and steady the lean man in black. Like her he had realized that pulling both triggers meant Wilson was holding an empty shotgun. But they both knew it also meant that if Caroline had so entertained Hustler and the coach driver that they hadn't caught Alice and Ramés's hurried exit through the window – unbelievable as that might sound – the shotgun's blast would have sounded a warning they couldn't ignore.

Sure enough, as Wilson struggled to pull out his ancient shooting iron, Hustler and the coach driver came tumbling out of the station's front door, six-guns flashing in the strengthening moonlight.

Caroline came tearing out after them. She stopped in the doorway, lifted her hideaway pistol with both hands and screamed a warning.

'Stop right there, both of you, let them go!'

Her words had no effect. Both men, federal marshal and coach driver, continued running towards the corral.

Caroline's pistol cracked. The muzzle flash was weak, the puff of smoke puny by comparison with that from larger weapons. But the result was dramatic.

The coach driver screamed in agony and went down, clutching his thigh. Hustler was disconcerted. He pulled up, and half turned. Trying to watch Alice and Ramés while seeing what was going on behind him, he ended up doing neither to the full.

The little pistol cracked again. The blow from the tiny chunk of lead turned Hustler the other way. He grabbed at his right shoulder. The pistol in his right hand drooped. Then the marshal recovered. His bloody left hand came away from his shoulder. He used it to grasp his right wrist. With that additional strength he was able to raise the big Peacemaker. He pointed it towards Caroline, and pulled the trigger.

Caroline Chauvin was knocked backwards. Her body twisted. She slammed into the door frame. Even from yards away Alice could hear the gasp as all the air was expelled from her lungs. The hideaway pistol fell into the dust. The young woman slid down the door frame and sat slumped against the rotting timber. In the moonlight, her eyes were pools of darkness.

It was as if the moment was frozen. Nobody moved. The coach driver was lying on his side, moaning. Hustler was like a statue, hand on right wrist, pistol still levelled.

Alice felt sick. She took a deep breath. Then, knowing that to quit would turn Caroline's self-sacrifice into a futile gesture of defiance, she shook herself mentally and flung a glance towards Ramés.

'She's given us the chance, Dom, so let's take it.'

This time Ramés needed no prompting. Using the reins as a handy quirt, he whipped the pony into motion. In ten yards the startled horse was at full gallop, in thirty it was little more than a cloud of dust swirling beyond the stationary coach and disappearing in a southerly direction.

Do something to confuse them, Alice thought. As Hustler at last turned unsteadily towards the corral she spurred her horse, tore through the gate and pointed its head towards the north. Not the way she wanted to go, she figured ruefully, but with Hustler having to rely for his pursuit on a coach with no driver and she and Ramés heading in opposite directions, they'd seized the initiative with both hands and there was damn all the federal marshal could do about it.

She gritted her teeth and concentrated on her riding. Her face, flushed with excitement, was cooled by the wind. The futile cracks of the frustrated marshal's belated and pointless shooting faded as the horse's pounding hoofs ate up the ground. After a while the steady rhythm of that headlong gallop grew soporific. Knowing that pursuit was almost impossible, Alice pulled the horse back to an easy canter. She sat up. Suddenly the breeze felt too cool, and she shivered. And now the slower pace allowed unwanted thoughts to surface.

What the wounded Hustler could do, Alice thought bitterly, was hang on to Caroline Chauvin – if she lived – and make sure he reached Topeka with at least one prisoner. Then she corrected herself: that was what the federal marshal could *try* to do.

With Caroline's help she and Ramés had already proved that prisoners were not sacks of grain, not lumpen beings to be moved from one place to another without protest. Their successful break meant that there were now three of them on the loose. Though she had been worried about Jean Pierre Boudreaux, instinct was telling her that whatever he had done he would eventually hold to their agreement and return to the hollow.

Ramés would do the same – had already made a move in the right direction because the hollow lay to the south.

Alice took a deep breath. That was it, then. They would meet there, at the hollow, the three of them – and then they would ride north in pursuit of the coach and make sure that Caroline Chauvin's sacrifice had not been in vain.

With a lightness in heart that she had not felt since their capture in the Coffeyville alley, Alice eased the horse in a gentle half circle and headed south.

NINE

'You been in this office before now?' Gatlin said softly. There was a rasp to his voice from breathing and swallowing too much black smoke. He smothered a cough, tried to clear his throat without making a noise then grimaced at his own foolishness. They'd just pushed he door open. If Boudreaux was in there he wasn't fool enough to believe it had been done by a gentle evening breeze.

Pine nodded his head at his question. 'In the office, yes, but no further.'

'Neither have I. For all we know, there could be a back way out.'

'Right. Boudreaux could have come in the front door and gone straight on through. You hear someone riding up the street in a hurry, you'll know we're too late – again.'

'All I can hear,' Gatlin said, 'is a crowd gathering out there and men who've been dragged from their beds organizing a chain of water buckets to fight two fires that could threaten the whole town.'

The two Pinkerton agents were standing well back and

out of any possible line of fire from the half-open door leading into the cell block. Their clothes stank of smoke. Both men were continually clearing their throats and struggling to hold back coughs. They had run straight through the flames in the hotel's lower hallway, covering their faces with their forearms, closing their eyes against the heat and running blind.

When they hit the plank walk it was Charlie Pine who had spotted the man running into the jail. He had jumped to the immediate and obvious conclusion: Boudreaux had set the fire as a diversion, and to trap Dusty Miller in the hotel; he now believed he was about to stage a heroic rescue mission and walk out of the jail with the three prisoners.

Instead, he had walked straight into the trap set for him by Marshal Dusty Miller. When the two Pinkerton men entered the jail, the trap snapped shut.

The oil lamp on the office desk was struggling to compete with the increasing light from the flames that was flickering on the walls and sending shadows dancing wildly about the small room. That light was to some extent helping the two agents: timber in the livery barn and the hotel was now being devoured by the hungry flames and, as they periodically flared high in the air, the illumination flooded the cell block. But only so far. Those brief bursts of bright light revealed a section of floor, the bars of those cells that could be seen from the door.

It was not enough.

Gatlin was holding a Winchester rifle he had taken from Miller's gun rack. A shell was in the breech. Now he waggled the gleaming weapon, indicating the cell block.

'We're pretty damn certain he's still in there,' he said.

'That being the case, you've got to go in and get him.'

'Me?'

'You've got the experience. I'm still a greenhorn at this game. But don't worry, I'll be right behind you.'

'You don't know how reassuring that is,' Pine said.

The banter was the way they worked. The words meant little. Both men were thinking hard. A jail was built with security in mind, so they didn't seriously believe there was a back way out.

'Maybe Boudreaux is still in there,' Pine said. 'But so's Miller. He was lying in wait. What the hell's gone wrong?'

Gatlin was frowning.

'We didn't hear a shot.'

'No. But remember New Orleans. When he murdered that couple, Boudreaux used a knife.'

'You think he could overpower Miller?'

'We know something's happened. Boudreaux went in. He's not come out. We know Miller was waiting in one of the cells. So now there's two of them in there, and all we've got is silence.'

Gatlin nodded.

'The cells are constructed of bars we can see through. There's nowhere for Boudreaux to hide.'

The flickering light from the flames consuming two of Coffeyville's principal buildings cast Pine's shadow large on the office walls as he went to the desk and reached the oil lamp. He turned up the wick. The flame spluttered, steadied. He held the lamp high.

'We could steal Boudreaux's idea. He created a diversion. There's not much in that cell block that will burn. We could toss this in. It'll smash on that floor. The

85

noise, the flames, it'll be one hell of a shock. I can't see any other way of going in there without getting our heads shot off. If it worked for Boudreaux. . . .'

They had been talking in undertones for what seemed an age, yet Gatlin knew the time they had wasted could be measured in just a few minutes. But that delay in itself would have set Boudreaux's nerves jangling. His heart would be pounding, his palms sweating, his mouth dry, his eyes staring in the gloom.

'Do it,' Gatlin said.

'And wait for Boudreaux to come out, or go in after the lamp?'

'Hang back. See what develops.'

Pine stepped forward. Gatlin stood to one side, held the Winchester high. Pine hefted the lamp. It felt full. He unscrewed the filler cap in the tin base, then shook the lamp so that oil spilled out. Then he drew back his arm and tossed the lamp into the cell block.

It flew in a high arc, tumbling in the air, spraying coal oil. It landed with a crash. The glass shattered. Coal oil began pouring from the open filler cap. The pool ignited. Flames flared, rising from the pool and flickering along the trail of spilled oil that led back to the door.

'Look there, on the floor,' Gatlin said hoarsely.

The smoky light was illuminating the room, the table, the barred cells. In front of the table, a man lay on the floor. He was on his back, arms spread wide. The burning pool of oil was spreading. The flames had reached the body and were already licking at the man's shirt.

'It's Miller,' Charlie Pine said, panic in his voice. 'Go, Jim, go.'

Drawing his six-gun, he obeyed his own desperate command and charged into the burning room.

Boudreaux had waited, and waited. The door remained half open. The ticking seconds had become minutes – and still nothing happened. But the delay was coming to his aid, giving him desperate thinking time. He was down on one knee waiting for the inevitable assault, but the instinct for survival was strong and suddenly his agile mind came up with a plan. He almost grinned: Alice didn't think much of his plans, and so far she'd been proved right. But this one *had* to work – or he was as good as dead.

The cell where Miller was lying was against the wall to Boudreaux's left. It was the nearest cell to the door. With the door in its present position, that cell could not be seen from the office.

Boudreaux holstered his six-gun. Working quickly and silently he went into the cell and dragged the unconscious Dusty Miller off the cot. Miller was a big man. He landed heavily. His head hit the floor with a bony crack. Blood spattered the hard-packed earth.

Boudreaux took hold of the marshal's ankles. Grunting, he dragged him out of the cell and placed him on the floor between the table and the door. A quick glance towards the door told him he hadn't been seen. He went back into the cell and stripped the blanket from the cot. This time when he left the cell he turned to face the bars. Then he draped the blanket around his neck, and began to climb. He climbed so that he was several feet above the floor. There he turned. He clung on, facing outwards. Risking a fall, he pulled the blanket from around his neck. He held it by a fold, shook it loose, let it hang.

A matador's cape, Boudreaux thought, remembering picture books from his school-days. But this one was not to distract a bull, nor was it for show.

He was clinging to the bars, a fly on the wall, when an object came hurtling in through the door. It hit the floor, shattered, and suddenly flames were spreading in all directions from a battered oil lamp. Eyes narrowed against the billowing black smoke, Boudreaux watched the fire begin to lick at Miller's clothing – and he couldn't believe his luck.

With a bang the door was dragged all the way open and a man charged into the room. He was holstering his six-gun. Boudreaux knew he would go for the helpless town marshal and drag him from the flames. A second man was close behind him. He was holding a rifle.

In that split second, with both men still close together, Boudreaux threw the blanket with a twist of the wrist and dropped from the bars.

He was drawing his six-gun as he landed. His throw had set the blanket whirling horizontally. For an instant it seemed to float in the smoke above the flames. Then it dropped over the two Pinkerton men, enveloping them from head to waist.

One of them roared in anger. The other used the Winchester to try to poke the blanket off his face. They were dancing in the flames. Their frantic efforts to get free were having the wrong effect. The two men collided. Suddenly they were entangled in the blanket's clinging folds.

Boudreaux stepped in close. Two vicious blows to their heads with the six-gun finished the men. They fell across the unconscious Miller, wrapped in the blanket. The smothered flames died away, then burst into life. The smell of burning cloth was strong in the room.

Boudreaux ran for the door. He pushed it to behind him. The key was in the lock. He looked at it, then turned away: fighting for his freedom was one thing, but he was not a murderer.

In the office he reached up to grab two gun-belts from the wall peg – Caroline's and Dom Ramés's. Then he looped them over his shoulder and ran into the street.

It was crowded. Men and women gathered on both plank-walks were watching in grim silence. They were lit up by the flaring, roaring flames. Across the street, teams of sweating, smoke-blackened men were fighting the fires. They were passing buckets from hand to hand. At the head of the line, men working with those full buckets were covering their faces and working as close to the fire as they could, swinging the bucket in an arc so that the water spread out in a sheet to blacken the flames, then grabbing the next bucket to repeat the process.

Unnoticed, Jean Pierre Boudreaux strolled along the plank walk away from the fires. He turned into the alley between 8th and 9th Streets and walked up to collect his horse.

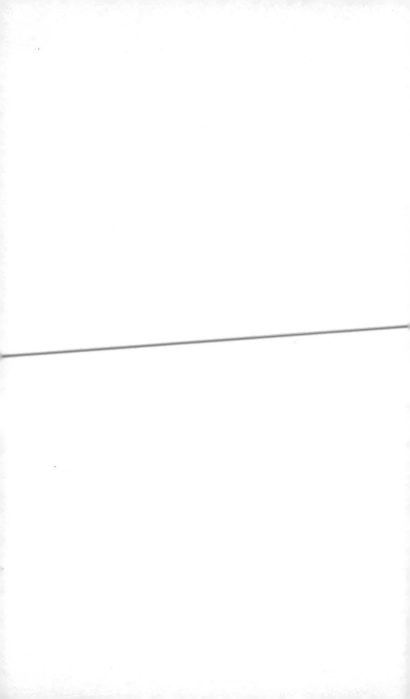

PART TWO

TEN

Midnight was two hours in the past when Dom Ramés rode the twisting northern path down through the mesquite into the hollow and along the silver ribbon of the Elk River to the moonlit campsite. There he quickly gathered kindling and started a fire. When flames and sparks were leaping beneath the trees and setting the leaves dancing in the heat, he hung his coffee pot over the blaze and sat back against the bole of a tree to consider his options.

His horse was grazing in the lush grass along the river bank. Ramés had loosened the girth, but not completely removed the rig because it was in his mind that he would soon be riding on. He had no idea what had planted that notion in his head. Probably, he decided, it was the disaster that had befallen them in Coffeyville, and the later brush with death at Wilson's station. It had occurred to him then – when he was staring death in the face – that Jean Pierre Boudreaux's problems were not his but could be made to work for him, and on the ride south to the hollow he had begun seriously questioning his own sanity.

Pouring coffee into a tin cup, sipping at the hot liquid and staring into the surrounding circle of darkness, Ramés freely admitted that he had experienced genuine fear when they'd been trapped in the Coffeyville alley. Fear had clamped its icy fingers on his heart once again when he and the two women had been marched from the jail and herded into the old Concord coach.

It was the same weakening, gripping fear that had followed him from New Orleans. He did not consider himself a coward, despite Caroline Chauvin's cruel suggestion. He had been experiencing the natural fear of discovery, of exposure and what would follow, and that fear had driven him to complain to Boudreaux about the proposed bank raid, to point out that the venture was foolhardy in the extreme – to beg him to abandon the idea, without actually putting that plea into words.

Those unspoken entreaties had been made to Jean Pierre Boudreaux, and therein lay a terrible irony. Jean Pierre, the man planning a daring bank robbery, was a man on the run accused of a savage murder. Yet, six months earlier, he had been there when Dom Ramés was himself in trouble and desperately seeking a way out.

Oh, Ramés freely admitted that, for him, trouble had always been a way of life. He had grown up in New Orleans, had made his living there by cheating at cards, stealing from the weak and using his considerable charm to tempt vulnerable ladies to part with their cash. But nothing in his character or in his previous behaviour had suggested that one night he would commit a serious crime. Indeed, on that dark night in New Orleans there had been a feeling of detachment, of standing back and

94

observing dispassionately a man to whom he had no connection.

Later that night, cowering in his room, he had been paralysed with fear. The next day he was terrified to venture out into the daylight. He had done so – but only with immense effort.

Twenty-four hours later he had been handed a lifeline. He was approached by a casual acquaintance, Jean Pierre Boudreaux. Boudreaux was wanted for the murder of two old people in Bourbon Street. Although he swore he was innocent – in Ramés's experience, they all did – he was on the run and had to leave New Orleans in a hurry. Mutual friends had agreed to go with him: Alice LaClaire and Caroline Chauvin. They would head for Baton Rouge, cross the Sabine river into Texas then head north.

Would Dom Ramés, Boudreaux asked, like to go with them?

Ramés sent the dregs of his coffee hissing into the flames then lit a cigarette. He was still undecided. Common sense told him he should sit and wait. The plan, if the bank robbery went wrong, had been to meet back at the campsite. Caroline had taken a bullet from Hustler's big six-gun and was unlikely to survive. Jean Pierre had slipped out of the trap in the alley and was almost certainly on the loose, and Ramés was pretty sure he'd seen Alice LaClaire riding like a bat out of hell away from Wilson's station. Riding in the wrong direction but Ramés had no doubt that, once she was clear, she'd turn south and head for the hollow.

Jean Pierre had been free from the start, had slipped

away from the gunfight in the alley and had never been caught. That thought reminded Ramés of another element in Boudreaux's plan: if any of them were caught, those still free would attempt a rescue. Miller had effectively ruled that out by moving the prisoners. But had Boudreaux been watching, and seen them board the coach? Or had he gone straight from the alley to the hollow?

Ramés flicked ash from the cigarette, his eyes narrowed in thought. He imagined a change of role: Jean Pierre had been caught, he, Ramés, had got away. What would he have done?

Before anything, he'd have stashed the money. No point beginning an attempt at a jail break by riding into Coffeyville, or anywhere else, on a horse bearing saddle-bags stuffed with cash stolen from the First National Bank. So, Boudreaux would have hidden the money. The best, the only place to stash it, was right there in the campsite.

But where was Boudreaux now?

Ramés sat up straight. Where he was didn't matter, so long as he stayed away for a while. For suddenly, with a feeling of immense relief, a half-hour of muddled thinking had been replaced by clarity. More than that, he realized that something that had been niggling away at the back of his mind suddenly made sense.

He had prepared the kindling, lit the fire, brewed coffee. He had done all that without giving any significance to something that had been staring him in the face: the stones encircling the fire had been disturbed.

Not randomly disturbed. Deliberately rearranged.

Dom Ramés climbed to his feet and began to prowl. He

looked at the stones from every angle; narrowed his eyes so that they were slightly out of focus and he saw, not individual stones, but the way they were grouped. At once he could see that the disturbed stones – just three or four of them – would, if fully formed, be recognizable as a crude arrowhead pointing towards the woods.

Damn right they would, he thought gleefully.

Careless of the heat he reached into the fire and pulled out a blazing brand. Holding it high, he walked up the slope. Now, by the light of the flickering flames, he could see the gleam of white at the edge of the woods where several branches had been snapped off. Ahead, deeper in the woods, at the extreme limits of the light, there was a fallen tree.

Ramés's jaw tightened. Twigs crackled underfoot as he moved closer and saw the naked roots nature had torn from the earth; saw the covering of leaves and earth that screamed of human interference.

He dropped to his knees, rammed the end of the blazing brand into the earth and began digging among the dead roots like a dog burying a bone. Loose earth flew. Within seconds the light from the blazing torch was shining on leather.

Ramés lunged with both hands into the loose earth, then sat back on his heels. He was clutching Jean Pierre Boudreaux's packed saddle-bags. He closed his eyes, his mind whirling. The leather was cold, slick with damp. Beneath the supple leather his fingers could feel the outline of the bundled bank notes. What had Boudreaux said? Five thousand dollars?

Ramés opened his eyes. Then he swallowed. The clarity

that had come to him at the camp-fire had been blown away by his discovery. He had accurately followed Boudreaux's movements. He had followed the trail Boudreaux had left, and he had found the saddle-bags containing the money.

But now what should he do?

ELEVEN

Coughing, spluttering, eyes streaming, Jim Gatlin rolled away from the smoke and flames and struggled to his feet. Agony shot though his skull as he straightened up and looked about him.

Charlie Pine was up on his knees, a phoenix rising from the flames. Gatlin leaped forward. He stripped the smoking blanket from his partner's shoulders, pushed Pine out of the way and used the blanket as a fire beater on the crawling flames. The coal oil was thick, slow to burn on the naked earth floor, easy to extinguish. Under Gatlin's steady beating, the flames quickly died. From the dying flames black smoke rose thickly, swirling across the floor, curling up through the office door.

'Miller's still out,' Pine said hoarsely.

Together the two Pinkerton men took hold of the unconscious marshal and dragged his dead weight across the hot, smoking floor. He groaned, opened his eyes and began weakly flapping his arms as they bumped him into the cooler, clearer air in the office. Somehow they heaved his bulk up so that he was lolling in his swivel chair, arms dangling. He took several deep breaths, then leaned forward and dropped his head into his hands.

'I feel the same way,' Jim Gatlin said.

Pine merely nodded. He'd dropped into another chair, and had turned a sickly green.

Gatlin went to the street door and peered out.

'Those big fires're under control, but that's about the only positive. All that's left of the barn and the hotel are two heaps of blackened timber.' He frowned. 'We couldn't have been out that long – could we?'

'Any longer,' Pine said, 'and we'd have been fried beef.'

'Our own fault. I guess throwing that lamp was a foolish idea.'

'Mine, as I recall, but we both agreed.'

Gatlin turned from the door, his face grim.

'Foolish or not, in the end it made no difference. Boudreaux's been a jump ahead of us from the word go. The way that blanket fell he must have been hanging on the bars. He threw it like a cowboy roping a steer, and followed it with his six-gun swinging.'

'Yeah,' Pine said, gingerly rubbing his head, 'and I can still feel that steel hitting bone.'

Gatlin grinned. 'Knocked some sense into us, you think?'

'If it has, it's way too late – Boudreaux's long gone.'

There was a thump as Dusty Miller leaned forward and dropped his forearms on the desk. He was having difficulty holding his head up. His eyes were heavy and unfocused.

'I lay on a cot and looked that feller in the eye,' he said, his voice thin. 'Last I remember is a six-gun heading for my skull. If your idea was foolish, me deciding to lie in wait for him was plain stupid. At the very least I should have kept Tom Bellard here with me, hidden somewhere so he could spring out if things went wrong.'

'I think I saw Tom out there,' Gatlin said.

'Yeah, he would be. If I know Tom he'll have taken charge of the fire fighting.'

'Well, you know why we're after Boudreaux because it was you spotted him and wired the Pinkertons,' Gatlin said. 'He's a killer. Where we went wrong was assuming that meant he was lacking in intelligence. We paid the price and now we're back where we were a couple of weeks ago.'

Miller grunted. He climbed to his feet, wincing and narrowing his eyes as he lifted his head.

'Maybe it's not as bad as you make out. You talked about positives, and I can see some. Three bank robbers are on their way to stand trial in Topeka. That's something I got right.'

'Yeah, and we're only back where we started,' Charlie Pine pointed out, 'if that was Boudreaux setting fire to those buildings and leaving us looking like circus clowns. What d'you reckon, Miller? You got a close look from that cosy bed you were lying in. Was it Boudreaux?'

The big marshal had stepped gingerly from behind the desk and had made it as far as the door Gatlin had left open. He was leaning against the frame, sucking in deep breaths of the cool night air.

'Well, the man who knocked me out was the same man I saw across the street from the bank a week ago, the same man I saw sitting in Frank Deakin's office smoking one of his fat cigars while he waited for the clerk to hand him five thousand dollars. Also, the weapons I took from Ramés and that dark-haired woman are no longer hanging on the peg so, puttin' it all together, yeah, it was Boudreaux all right.'

'Then after what he attempted here,' Pine said, 'I don't have to tell either of you where he is now.'

Gatlin had dragged a chair away from the wall and was straddling it with his arms folded on the back. At Pine's words he nodded thoughtfully.

'Not realizing they'd been moved, he went to a lot of wasted effort to get his pals out of jail. He's not going to give up after one setback. He knows they're not here, so he'll be working out the most likely places for them to be taken. Coffeyville's just an old man's tired spit from the Oklahoma border, so they won't have been taken south. If he knows his geography he'll quickly realize Topeka's close to the penitentiary at Lansing – and that makes the capital the obvious place to take them.'

'Then he's got some catching up to do,' Miller said. 'Jake Hustler's got some twelve hours' start on him.'

Gatlin pulled a face. 'Maybe, but the coach'll be forced to stop overnight. They're heading north from Coffeyville. Knowing the time they set out and the distance the coach team can take them before dark, where's Hustler likely to pull them off the trail?'

'Wilson's station,' Miller said.

'So they bed down there, rise at sun-up, eat breakfast. By the time Hustler moves them out, Boudreaux could be closing fast.'

'And if we set off now,' Pine said, 'we'll be right behind

him. The Pinkertons do it again, another desperate criminal apprehended—'

'Rider coming,' Miller said from the door. 'If my eyes ain't deceiving me, it's the man who calls himself Dom Ramés.'

TWELVE

With the stink of smoke in his nostrils and the cries of the men fighting the fires ringing in his ears, Jean Pierre Boudreaux had collected his horse from the alley, left the stolen horses tied to the broken fence and was halfway between Coffeyville and the camp in the hollow when he decided to pull off the trail and into the trees to rest the big bay.

The horse wasn't alone in needing a breather. Boudreaux had spent most of the ten miles or so he'd covered since leaving Coffeyville in trying to work out what had happened to Ramés and the two women. So many possibilities had presented themselves that, when he swung out of the saddle and stepped away from the horse to light a cigarette, his brain felt as if it had been overheated then fried by the fires he had set in the barn and the hotel.

The cigarette smoke he drew into his lungs, the soft moonlight, the restful sound of trees whispering in the gentle breeze – all of these helped to steady his nerves and clear his head. Eventually, sitting down with his back to a tree, he realized that there were really only two possibilities: the prisoners had been moved to another location in Coffeyville, or they'd been moved out of the town. The first gave him the opportunity for a second try at tearing them away from the arms of the law. The second left him looking at an impossible task.

As if a logjam had been unblocked, thoughts were now flowing freely. The idea that he could be looking at an exhausting spell chasing the impossible had him asking himself the obvious question: why bother? He had already burned down half a town in his efforts to honour the agreement they had made. To keep trying now risked getting nothing at all from a well-planned and perfectly executed bank robbery. True, after leaving the bank things had gone badly wrong, and Ramés and the two women were left contemplating a long spell in jail – which was enough to drive a person crazy. But Boudreaux knew that, if he was in their position, those long years in a cramped cell would be a lot easier to get through if he had the satisfaction of knowing the robbery that had put him there had succeeded; that at least one of them had got clear away.

In any campaign, casualties are expected. The outcome is judged not on the number who have fallen, but on the objective, and the result. Their aim had been to rob a bank, and Boudreaux had $5,000 of the First National money safely stashed away.

Ten minutes later, still deep in thought as he stood up and flicked his cigarette stub into the dust, he was shocked to see Dom Ramés ride straight past him in the thin moonlight.

*

Boudreaux's first thought was that he was seeing a ghost, his immediate impulse to holler out to his friend.

But there was something about Ramés as the lean man in black came cantering by that caused Boudreaux to hold his tongue. Trees lined the trail, and Ramés was alternately in light and shade, seen clearly then seen only as a black shape against the even darker trees. But it was in one of those moments when a shaft of moonlight slanted through a gap in the trees to cast its pale light over the lone rider that Boudreaux realized what had caught his eye and stayed his tongue.

Dom Ramés was riding towards Coffeyville, and he was taking with him the saddle-bags Boudreaux had last seen wedged beneath the roots of the fallen tree as he covered the old leather with earth and dead leaves.

Silently, Boudreaux mounted up and moved out onto the trail. He turned to follow Ramés, keeping far enough back and deep enough in shadow to avoid detection, close enough so that there was no risk of losing the night rider.

As he rode, there was a frown on his face. Seeing Ramés had been shock enough, because Boudreaux had already decided the prisoners had been moved from the jail to a more secure location. If he was right, then Ramés had somehow escaped. He'd made it to the hollow and found the money, which had been Boudreaux's intention when he left the sign. But where were the women? Where was Ramés going now, and why was he taking the money with him?

The flicker of moonlight through the trees was

disorientating. Dazed by events that seemed to be moving too fast and out of control, Boudreaux felt dizzy. He was having difficulty concentrating. Wild thoughts were chasing each other through a mind that seemed to be losing its grasp on reality.

Eventually, struggling to get to grips with the situation while keeping an eye on the mounted figure riding ahead of him, Boudreaux was forced to admit that his thinking was muddled because he was refusing to admit the obvious: Dom Ramés, the man who had ridden with him from New Orleans, was riding to Coffeyville to return the stolen money to the bank.

But was that so unexpected? Ramés had come across the group as a stranger, and pleaded a need to get out of town. Caroline Chauvin had never trusted him. And at one point before the bank robbery he had seemed to be goading Boudreaux into returning to New Orleans to face the music.

Why would he do that?

Yet even as Boudreaux allowed unpleasant and confusing thoughts to battle it out under the surface, it seemed he was wrong to put the man's actions down to simple betrayal.

Ramés had turned off the trail. Boudreaux eased his horse close and pulled into the trees. He watched Ramés slip from the saddle. In a patch of bright moonlight the man in black unbuckled the saddle-bags and carried them into the undergrowth. Minutes later he emerged, slapping his empty hands on his pants. He looked about him, as if committing the scene to memory. Then he reached up and ripped a young branch from a tree, leaving a white

107

scar that gleamed in the moonlight.

He mounted up and rode out onto the trail. A last look backwards seemed to convince him that the white scar was a marker he couldn't miss. With a satisfied nod he put spurs to his horse and cantered off in the direction of Coffeyville.

It took Boudreaux less than five minutes to recover the saddle-bags. After a quick check to make sure the money was all there he sat back on his haunches and did some fast thinking. All right, so the man liked playing games. Well he, Boudreaux, also enjoyed a bit of fun – especially if it might lead to an interesting conclusion. Smiling to himself in the darkness, he emptied both bags and buried them again. Then he took off his jacket and, using a rawhide thong, created a crude sack in which he stowed all the money. That done he strapped it behind the big bay's saddle and once again turned onto the trail and headed towards the hollow.

But now he rode with a lighter heart. He had been facing the possibility that his partners in crime had been moved somewhere out of his reach to await trial, had even contemplated taking the money and leaving them to their fate. Ramés's sudden appearance had changed all that.

If Ramés was free, then it was likely that Caroline Chauvin and Alice LaClaire had also got away. If so, then they would have stuck to the plan and made for the hollow. Once there, they were faced with a problem. Just as he, Boudreaux, had known nothing of their whereabouts, or what had happened to them, so they had no idea where he was or what he had been doing. Then they had found the money. There would have been a heated discussion: sit tight, wait for Boudreaux to turn up – or take off with the money while there was still time.

It seemed that Dom Ramés had decided the only way out of the mess was to give himself up and hope the law took that gesture into account when he was sentenced. But he was also keeping a hole card, a bargaining chip: the money, which he would hand over to the authorities in Coffeyville when the bargain was signed and sealed. Either that, or he was going to place the blame for everything squarely on his, Boudreaux's, shoulders, and return years later to collect the cash when he'd finished his spell in jail.

He had been riding to town on his own. That suggested both women had hotly disagreed with his plan, and had opted to remain where they were and wait for Boudreaux.

The conviction that the two women were waiting for him in the hollow spurred Boudreaux on. But as the miles fell away beneath the big bay's pounding hoofs, his mood changed yet again. With his mind constantly returning furiously to Ramés's betrayal, he quickly came to realize that the authorities in Coffeyville would not be satisfied even if Ramés did allow them to recovery of the money. They would want the bank robbers – every damn one of them.

Dom Ramés, fighting to save his own neck from the hangman's noose, wouldn't hesitate. He'd give them exactly what they wanted.

That thought was still haunting Boudreaux with its implications when the big bay faltered and went lame.

THIRTEEN

Gatlin had joined Miller at the door when Ramés rode through the smoke hanging in the moonlit street and, watched without interest by the exhausted fire-fighters, turned in towards the jail. The Pinkerton man signalled to Pine then stepped outside and walked a few yards away from the door before turning to await developments. Miller followed suit; he placed himself on the other side of the door, facing Gatlin.

Ramés, lean and dark in dusty black clothing, swung out of the saddle and tied his lathered horse at the rail. Then he turned, cast a fleeting glance at the ruined buildings on the other side of the road and sprang up onto the plank walk. He looked hard at the marshal and the Pinkerton man, grinned arrogantly and shook his head as he walked straight into the office. Gatlin threw Miller a puzzled glance, then without haste the two of them followed Ramés inside.

Ramés had stopped just over the threshold. He was looking at Charlie Pine. Still sitting relaxed in the chair,

110

Pine had his six-gun out. His hand was on his knee, the six-gun pointing nowhere but presenting an implied and potent threat.

'Your partner's taken your gunbelt,' Pine said, 'but if you're carrying any hidden weapons, get rid of them now.'

Ramés raised his arms from his sides, palms turned to Pine, then let them fall. He cocked his head.

'My partner's got my gunbelt? Are you saying Boudreaux's been here?'

'He's the man set fire to the livery barn and the hotel. His aim was to release you and the two women. As you know, he was too late because you'd been moved out.'

'But he came here, and he got away.' Ramés looked at the three lawmen and shook his head. 'I detect heavy heads, assorted bruises. And by the stink in here he splashed some more coal oil around before noticing the empty cells.'

'Which is now history,' Miller said, 'and what happened in even the recent past isn't going to worry me too much if, one by one, you're all going to ride in and give yourselves up.' He narrowed his eyes thoughtfully. 'I take it you all got away from Hustler?'

'Just me and Alice. We made the break at Wilson's station. Caroline Chauvin made it possible, but while helping us she took a slug that's probably finished her. I tried to make that sacrifice in her place,' he lied, 'but she wouldn't listen.' Then he grinned. 'Is that what you think this is? Me walking in to give myself up?'

'You're here, you're heading for a cell – you got any other reasonable explanation?'

While talking Miller had taken hold of Ramés's

111

shoulder. Now he put his weight behind his hand and began to turn Ramés towards the door at the back of the room.

Ramés shook him off. Miller brought his other hand across and gripped the back of Ramés's shirt. Gatlin quickly moved to the bank robber's other side, crowded him, knocking him off balance but content to let Miller do the running.

Bracing his legs, Ramés said quickly, 'Locking me up means saying a permanent goodbye to those five thousand dollars that went missing. You want that?'

Miller tightened his grip.

'Boudreaux's got that money.'

'Boudreaux *had* that money. Then he hid it. Then it was found. Then it went missing.'

'And you're about to tell us where it is, and buy your freedom?'

'Oh, I'm going to hand you much more than that,' Ramés said, 'if you back off and give me the time and the space.'

Miller shook his head. 'You're in no position to strike bargains.'

'Tell that to the Pinkertons up in Denver.'

'He doesn't need to go that far,' Gatlin said, stepping away from Ramés and closing the street door. 'Two of those Pinkerton men are in this room.'

Ramés raised his eyebrows.

'Well, well,' he said softly. 'And what's those Pinkerton men's views on what I'm offering?'

'You talk, we'll listen,' Gatlin said. He looked at Miller. 'There's nothing to lose. If we don't like what we hear, you

112

lock him up.'

Gatlin stood with his back to the door. He watched Miller, satisfied that there was no way out for Ramés, walk around the desk. Pots clattered as he busied himself setting coffee to brew on the big iron stove. Then he turned and dropped into his swivel chair.

'Even if we like what we hear I can still lock him up, and he knows it,' he said. 'The way these things work, he gets a promise from me – I let him walk free, he cops a reduced sentence, something like that – then he hands over the information and the money. The trouble is he's got to trust me and in these situations, to get what they want, both sides tend to lie through their teeth.'

'Similar thoughts crossed my mind long before I rode into town,' Ramés said. 'I was having second thoughts until I realized I was holding all the right cards. I can give you the money, I can give you Boudreaux.' He looked at Gatlin. 'Boudreaux's the killer the Pinkertons would love to get their hands on – right?'

'We've been looking for him, yes,' Gatlin conceded. 'But how do you know that? Do you *know* he's a vicious killer, a man who kills old folk? Has he *bragged* about it to the three of you?'

'It's no secret. But I still need to know what happens to me if I give you Boudreaux.'

Gatlin shrugged. 'Miller's the Coffeyville marshal, and it was Coffeyville's bank you robbed. What happens to you is in Miller's hands.'

'Maybe so, but I've just turned up a hole card I didn't even know I was holding,' Ramés said. 'The Pinkertons. That hole card is going to win me the pot, because the

113

Pinkertons surely won't allow a wanted killer to slip through their fingers because a small-town marshal wants his moment of glory.'

Gatlin saw Miller's jaw tighten at the insult.

'Say your piece, Ramés. State your terms, now, or get thrown into one of my cells.'

'There's another reason for me to talk fast. Something's telling me time could be on Boudreaux's side.'

Gatlin grimaced. 'So get on with it.'

Moving in a relaxed manner, clearly believing he had centre stage and had taken control, Ramés walked to one of the hard chairs and sat down. Gatlin remained by the door. Pine holstered his six-gun.

'Here's the situation,' Ramés said. 'We broke away from Hustler at Wilson's station, me and Alice LaClaire. The only horse left in the corral was a ragged nag with no saddle. Hustler had that old Concord he could climb into – useless for a pursuit – and to compound his difficulties we rode off in different directions. I headed south, made it back to the hollow—'

'Where's that?' Gatlin snapped.

'Twenty miles to the north-west of here, on the Elk River.'

'I know it,' Miller said. 'Damn it, is that where you four have been holed up?'

'Been camped there for a while before Boudreaux came up with his big idea of robbing a bank. When I got there tonight, it was deserted. I couldn't figure out where Boudreaux had gone. Now I know. But if he was here, and he got away, then he'll be making straight for the hollow because that's where he'd hidden the saddle-bags.'

114

'But you've moved them?'

'Damn right I have.'

'How come you didn't see Boudreaux? He must have been heading out of Coffeyville at the same time you were heading in.'

'Pure good luck. And I needed it. Until halfway to town I was carrying those bags, looking for the right place to hide them.'

'So when Boudreaux gets there and finds the money gone – what will he do?'

'Go crazy. He must have hidden the saddle-bags because he couldn't carry them with him when he rode back into Coffeyville on a rescue mission. I found them because he left sign for us to read – I suppose in case any of us made it back there and something had happened to him. But anyone could've read the sign, so anyone stumbling on the hollow could have found the cash. He'll realize he's slipped up, but when he calms down he'll know there's nothing he can do before daylight. So that's what he'll do next – nothing – he'll sit tight. He'll be there now, rolled up in his blankets by the camp-fire. If I know Alice, she'll eventually make it to the hollow. The two of them are real close, so her being there will make him feel better.'

'Get to the point,' Jim Gatlin said.

'Miller knows the hollow. You ride in nice and easy you'll probably catch them when they're sleeping.'

'And the money?'

For a few moments there was a tense silence. Miller pulled out a battered turnip watch and glanced at the time. Ramés was pursing his lips and seemed to be

THE SECOND COFFEYVILLE BANK RAID

thinking hard.

'Ramés, that money's your hole card, not the Pinkertons,' Gatlin said, breaking the silence as he took the initiative. 'By telling Miller about the hollow you've already given us your partners – if we move fast – but it's that stolen cash that's going to buy your freedom. Trouble is, trust is the only way a handover can be worked, and your problem is the one Miller described. We can give you our word, then double-cross you when we've got our hands on the money.'

Ramés frowned.

'How about this? You give me a gun, two of you back off a couple of hundred yards. I take one of you with me, unarmed, to where it's hidden. I hand over the cash, release him and ride off.'

'That's you giving your word, and how do we know we can trust you? Besides, it'd be foolish to hand you a gun. You could plug the man you take with you and ride off *with* the cash.'

'All right, so one of you holds me, two of you ride for the cash, signal, and I'm released—'

Gatlin grinned at the consternation on Ramés's face as the bank robber recognized the flaw and shut his mouth.

'We're back with trust, right?' Gatlin said quietly. 'Can't get away from it. You're banking on that man releasing you – and what if he decides not to?'

'And it's no good you telling us where the money's supposed to be, because we could ride off on a wild goose chase while you hightail it in the opposite direction – with the saddle-bags,' Charlie Pine said.

Another long silence. Miller poured four tin cups of

coffee and handed them around. All four men drank, Ramés deep in thought, Jim Gatlin watching him and knowing full well that there was no solution to the man's dilemma. Somehow Ramés had to hand the money over to buy his release, but he couldn't trust them to release him if he did.

'Forget the money for now,' Gatlin said. 'Let's go get Boudreaux.'

'That suits me,' Miller said. 'I've got Ramés.'

'Ramés?'

The lean man in black shook his head.

'No. I'm betraying friends. I want to be over the border into Oklahoma before you tackle Boudreaux.' He looked at Miller. 'Have we got an agreement? If you get those saddle-bags with the First National money, I go free?'

Miller frowned.

'You were part of that bank robbery, I *know* it, but you weren't anywhere near the bank so how can that be proved?' he said, musing aloud. 'You resisted arrest, but the only man who took a bullet was you, and a good lawyer would set out to prove you could've been waiting in that alley for any damn reason.' He took a deep, disgusted breath. 'You're already halfway to being a free man, because convicting you of anything is going to be one almighty chore. So, OK, you've got yourself a deal.'

'And you Pinkertons?'

'We're interested in Jean Pierre Boudreaux.' Gatlin shrugged. 'I told you, this is Miller's town. He says you go free, we'll go along with that.'

'And I can trust you?'

'Feller, there's nothing else you can do.'

Ramés grimaced, then nodded.

'All right, let's go get that money.'

FOURTEEN

The wire received by the telegraph operator in Coffeyville, Kansas, and handed to Marshal Dusty Miller, read:

To: Jim Gatlin, Charlie Pine,
From: James McParland, Superintendent Pinkerton Detective Agency, Western Division, Denver, Colorado.
Advise tread carefully. Possible doubt over Boudreaux's involvement in New Orleans killings. New eyewitness volunteered information in last couple of days. Saw man running from victims' apartment thirty minutes before Boudreaux left the apartment. Tall, lean, possibly carrying knife.
Also, think possible name of dead New Orleans couple may be of some use. It's Chauvin.

Miller sat in his office and read the message several times. Then he stared out of the window. He couldn't hand the message to the two Pinkerton men. They had left town with Dom Ramés who was going to lead them to the money. From there they would ride on to the hollow for a possible confrontation with the other bank robbers.

Miller sighed deeply, filed the message on a spike and reached for his hat.

FIFTEEN

Boudreaux could see the yellow light of the fire flickering under the trees as soon as he rode over the ridge and started the bay carefully down through the mesquite. He could see it, could smell the sweet, acrid smoke and, by God, it was so achingly familiar it felt almost like a homecoming. The half smile of pure pleasure was still lingering when he rode along the banks of the glittering Elk River and saw in the moonlight the glint of fair hair as Alice LaClaire came running to meet him.

He swung down from the bay and swept her into his arms, then held her away from him with his hands gripping her shoulders as he looked into her blue eyes.

'I reckon there's two sides of a long story to tell,' he said. 'I don't know where you've been but, as the saying goes, I've been to hell and back and got nothing for my troubles.'

'Even that's more than poor Caroline got for hers,' Alice said gravely. 'I think she's finished, probably dead, Pierre. And if she is she gave her life for me, and for Dom – a man she doesn't like or trust.'

'That's the way she was. All action. She was the one who wanted to break out of the alley, she was first to turn her horse and charge those armed men.'

Boudreaux had quickly loosened the saddle cinch and they were walking towards the camp-fire as they talked. At mention of Ramés's name he had snorted his contempt. Now Alice looked at him sharply. He pulled a face, dropped down onto a large flat stone by the fire and poured coffee into tin cups. One he handed to Alice, from the other he drank greedily.

'You go first,' he said.

He listened intently as, without wasting a word, Alice told him everything that had happened since the gunfight in the Coffeyville alley. Boudreaux shook his head and grimaced when she told him how the prisoners had been moved from the jail and forced onto a Concord coach bound for Topeka. He frowned and winced as she told him of Caroline Chauvin's part in the escape from Wilson's station and what had befallen the courageous young woman. When Alice went on to tell him how she and Ramés had split up to confuse Federal Marshal Jake Hustler, Boudreaux's face hardened.

'What?' Alice said. 'What's happened that I don't know about?'

Though Boudreaux knew that she was referring to Ramés, he quickly told her of his own escape from the alley and his subsequent violent attempt to rescue the prisoners he believed to be locked in cells the Coffeyville jail.

'I guess I went too far, put a lot of lives in danger with those fires I started,' he admitted as his story drew to a close. 'It's something I will regret for the rest of my life, but as far as I knew my pretty blonde-haired friend was in a prison cell and—'

He broke off, shrugging as the lump in his throat prevented him from talking.

Alice smiled. 'And you'd do anything for me, just as I've done everything for you and stuck by you since that horrible day in New Orleans when you found out you were wanted for a crime you did not commit.'

'And still wanted, still hunted,' Boudreaux said.

'But what about Dom? I mention his name, and your mood blackens. I know he's not the pleasantest of fellows, and back at Wilson's station Caroline told him to his face that she doesn't trust him – but what has he done, Pierre?'

'He's taken the bank money, hidden it—'

'What – you've seen him?'

'I've seen him, and he's been here, but he doesn't know that I've seen him.'

'Well, I knew for sure he was ahead of me. I swung north from Wilson's station, he headed south and was bound to get here before me. But if he's been here, then where is he now? And how can he have the money? I know you had it in your saddle-bags, and I saw when you rode in that you haven't got them now, just your blanket roll and jacket. So what have you done with them? – what has *Dom* done with them?'

'I hid them here before I rode off to rescue you like a knight in shining armour, but left sign anyone could read. Dom must have followed that sign and dug up the bags. He had them with him. When I saw him, he was heading for Coffeyville. I saw him stop to bury the saddle-bags, then continue on his way. I think he's going to talk to Marshal Miller, bargain with him.'

'Buy his freedom with the money?'

'He might try that, but he's doomed to failure. You were right about that bundle behind my saddle: it's my blanket roll and jacket. But inside that jacket there's the money we took from the First National bank. I recovered the saddle-bags, emptied them and put them back where I found them.'

Alice was beaming. 'Clever old you. But that doesn't mean Dom wasn't going to try to bargain with the money. He would do that, wouldn't he?'

'Not necessarily. There is another way.'

'I've got a horrible feeling I know where this is leading.'

'Yes. As far as anyone in Coffeyville knows, I got away, I've got the money. Ramés now believes *he's* got the money in a safe place. I think he'll try to hang on to that and give us to Miller in exchange for his freedom.'

'How will he do that?'

'Damn it, Alice, the plan was for us all to meet back here if there was trouble. Ramés knows you're heading this way, and he'll be damn sure I'm coming back because this is where I buried the money. All he's got to do is tell Miller about this hollow.'

'Oh my God.'

Alice had her hand to her mouth. Her eyes were huge.

'I think we've got some time,' Boudreaux said, with hasty reassurance he didn't feel. 'Like I said, Ramés was heading the opposite way when I saw him. He's got to ride to Coffeyville, then talk Miller around to his way of thinking. I think the marshal will take some convincing.'

124

'That doesn't mean we can hang around here. The more distance we put between us and them—'

'You're right,' Boudreaux cut in. 'We've got time, but not a lot of it because there's a problem.'

Alice took a deep breath. 'I thought things were going too well. Go on, what is it?'

'My horse went lame. I've nursed it, taken it very easy. At times I dismounted and walked to ease the load, but that means it took me too damn long getting here. Ramés will have gained time. He'll have reached Coffeyville and been talking to Miller while I was still on the trail. If the marshal made his mind up real fast – and that's always possible if Ramés makes an offer he couldn't refuse – then Miller and his deputy could have been closing on me while I was patiently nursing the horse.' He grinned mirthlessly. 'Make that *impatiently*. I was fretting every inch of the way, still am.'

'You say one thing, then another. You say we're safe – then you say we're not. So let's go, Pierre. Let's ride out now, before it's too late.'

But Boudreaux was up on his feet, walking away from the circle of firelight, his head cocked in an intent listening attitude.

Even while he and Alice were talking he had been careful to keep his ears tuned for any unusual sounds. At one point he had been convinced that he'd detected the crackle of distant gunfire, but couldn't imagine why that would be. Then, seconds ago, quite clear in the stillness of the night, he had heard a horse whicker. The sound had come from the south ridge above the twisting mesquite trail leading down into the hollow.

Now, as he drifted like a shadow towards the river bank, he heard an answering whinny. This sound had come from the north. It seemed that the men alerted by Dom Ramés had ridden very hard indeed from Coffeyville, their minds on the prize awaiting them. They had made it faster than Boudreaux could have imagined. Boudreaux knew that there were just two trails down into the hollow. He realized now that with the flickering camp-fire acting as a beacon, those men had swiftly and effectively sealed both ways in and out.

He and Alice LaClaire were prisoners. All they could do was sit and wait for the armed officers of the law to ride down and take them into custody.

Resistance would be futile. Yet what was the alternative? Nothing less than a lengthy term in a stinking prison cell. For himself, that was something he could bear. But for Alice LaClaire . . . ?

Gritting his teeth, Jean Pierre Boudreaux drew his six-gun. The cold steel glinted in the moonlight as he checked the loads. Then he looked up and spun the cylinder with a faint whirring sound that brought a soft exclamation of distress from Alice LaClaire.

SIXTEEN

Jim Gatlin took up the rear when he and Charlie Pine escorted Dom Ramés out of Coffeyville. Though the tall bank robber had made the decision to ride into town and offer a deal, Gatlin was still aware that the man could be lying through his teeth most of the time. On the face of it his offer was a good one, but old habits die hard. There seemed to be no point in his riding into town unless his offer was genuine, but it was always possible that beneath the placid surface of his good intentions a scheming mind was hard at work.

So, suspecting that Ramés was playing it straight but unable to empty his mind of nagging suspicion, Gatlin rode some thirty yards behind Ramés and Pine to give himself room and time to react if the bank robber made an unexpected move.

They proceeded in that manner for some fifteen miles, the moonlight turning the dust kicked up by the leading riders into a ghostly translucent veil through which Gatlin rode like a man in a dream. Indeed, that was the way he had felt for some time. Ever since his and Pine's arrival in

127

Coffeyville, events had unfolded in a bizarre fashion. Bank robbers had been captured, moved north, and allowed to escape. A section of the town had been burned down in an abortive attempt to rescue prisoners who were no longer in the cells. The man who had set the fires and stormed into the jail had been trapped, with no way out, yet still managed to fight his way to freedom. And now this. The money stolen from the First National bank was being returned, which left the town badly scarred by violence that had seen nothing lost, nothing gained. Apart from several burned buildings and bruised reputations, the town was as it had been before Jean Pierre Boudreaux and Alice LaClaire pulled up outside the First National bank in a fancy stolen buggy.

And both of them were still out there, a killer on the loose with his blonde-haired sidekick.

Gatlin's thoughts were abruptly terminated when, up ahead, Ramés lifted his arm and pulled his horse to a standstill. He was pointing to his right. As Gatlin drew closer he saw the white scar left when a branch had been ripped from a tree, and he guessed that this was Ramés's marker.

Charlie Pine glanced at Gatlin, then slid from the saddle. He waited for Ramés to do the same, then drew his six-gun and followed as the bank robber plunged into the ragged undergrowth under the trees. Pine held back. He saw Ramés drop to his knees. For a few moments the man in black dug furiously with both hands. Then, with an exclamation of triumph, he dragged two stained leather saddle-bags from the earth and held them aloft.

'Bring them out here,' Gatlin called.

But the bank robber had frozen. For a moment he sat back on his heels, staring at the dangling saddle-bags without moving. Then he hefted them, shook them; let them fall to the ground, bent over them and frantically unfastened the buckles and thrust his hands deep inside each bag in turn.

'It's gone.'

He scrambled to his feet and came crashing back through the undergrowth.

'The money was there in those bags, every last dollar – and now it's not. It's been taken—'

'Which means one thing,' Pine cut in. 'You didn't see Boudreaux, but he saw you all right – saw exactly what you were doing and moved in to recover the money when you continued on your way into town.'

'Then why did he leave the saddle-bags?'

Gatlin smiled. 'Warped sense of humour,' he said. 'He's sitting somewhere now, laughing fit to bust as he imagines the look on your face when you realize what he's done.'

'Damn him,' Ramés said softly.

'He's already damned by the crime he committed in New Orleans,' Pine said, 'but what this means is we've got to move fast. He watched you hide the money, recovered it as soon as you were out of the way and after that—'

'He'd head for the hollow,' Ramés said.

'Which is what we do now.'

'But without me.'

'Oh, no. The deal that was struck was dead as soon as you dug up those empty bags. You've been called, and the hand you've got to show is as worthless as a pair of deuces up against a full house. You didn't intend giving yourself

129

up when you rode in, but that's what you've done—'

'Rider coming,' Pine called.

In a flurry of movement both Pinkerton men moved off the trail, dragging Ramés with them. They slipped into the undergrowth. The agents covered their horses' muzzles with their palms, whispering soft words into pricked ears, soothing the animals with gentle hands. Pine had his six-gun jammed into Ramés's ribs. The bank-robber's eyes glittered. He was quivering with tension, a taut spring ready to snap.

'It's Tom Bellard,' Gatlin said. 'Miller's deputy.'

He stepped out onto the trail and waved the rider down. Startled, the deputy's horse reared backwards. Tom Bellard held him firmly while slapping a hand to his holstered six-gun. Then, recognizing Gatlin's face in the glint of moonlight, he relaxed.

'You gave me quite a start.'

'I could say the same. What brings you out this way?'

'A wire came through from your Denver office soon after you left town. Dusty reckons in the circumstances it's something you need to know in a hurry.'

He was reaching into his vest pocket as he spoke. Now he handed the crumpled slip of paper to the Pinkerton agent.

Gatlin read quickly, frowned. He looked across at Charlie Pine, waved the message slip.

'It's possible those New Orleans killings weren't done by Boudreaux.'

'Didn't McParland say Boudreaux's fingerprints were at the scene?'

'Oh, he was there at the old couple's apartment. But a

130

witness saw another man leaving the scene thirty minutes earlier.'

Silently, Gatlin handed the message slip to Pine. The shorter man read it carefully, the looked up at Gatlin with a glint in his eye.

'You see that name, Chauvin?'

'Sure. It rang a bell, but I couldn't place it—'

'Chauvin?' Dom Ramés said, thrusting forward, his eyes wide. 'What about Chauvin, what does it say about her?'

Gatlin frowned. 'Her?'

Tom Bellard was nodding. 'The dark-haired member of the gang is called Caroline Chauvin.'

'So what's going on?' Ramés blurted.

'Hold your horses,' Gatlin said. 'This says nothing about her. Chauvin is the name of that old couple Boudreaux murdered – or somebody murdered.'

'But it's interesting, nevertheless,' Charlie Pine said. 'Caroline has to be a tough young woman to get involved in a bank robbery—'

'She fought like a tiger in the alley,' Tom Bellard said.

'And if she left New Orleans with this group, immediately after the double killing. . . .'

'You mean if she's related to the old folk,' Gatlin said, 'this could have been a family killing?'

'Often works out that way,' Pine said, his face grim.

'If it was her did it,' Ramés said, sweat glistening on his face, 'it's way too late to do anything. I told you, she was gunned down at Wilson's station. That means you're not going to catch your New Orleans killer.'

Pine looked at Gatlin.

'So what now?'

'Well, Boudreaux may not be a killer, but he's still a wanted bank robber,' Tom Bellard pointed out.

'Yeah, and it'd be foolish to take as gospel information coming from a possibly unreliable witness six months after the murders,' Gatlin said. 'Like Tom said, Boudreaux's a bank robber. Also, we know he was in that murdered couple's apartment, so we need to talk to him to get that cleared up once and for all. Nothing's changed. We head for the hollow, fast as we can.'

'Tom,' Pine said, 'are you going with us, or does Miller need you back in town?'

'He said nothing to me. Just deliver the message.'

'Right, well, Ramés is officially your prisoner. He has to go with us—'

'No, I've done my bit, Deputy Bellard here must know the location of the hollow.'

'You've done nothing, given us nothing except a point on the map,' Gatlin said. To Bellard he said, 'Ride with us, Tom, and watch this man like a hawk. With you taking care of him it leaves us free to deal with whatever these bank robbers decide to throw our way.'

'Desperate men resort to desperate measures,' Charlie Pine warned as they moved out on the trail. 'What makes it worse is this man's got a woman with him.'

SEVENTEEN

The drunken poker players had been living up to a jealously guarded reputation. Regulars at Wilson's station, they had been known to continue a game of five-card stud when the winter winds were howling across the Kansas plains, the roof of the old building was being ripped away shingle by shingle and the only light in the low-slung building came from guttering candles that flickered on the greasy cards in gloved hands.

This calm night, six shots had been fired. Three slugs had hit home and some blood had been shed. But nobody had died and, other than watching with mild interest as Ramés and Alice LaClaire made their daring escape, the poker players had concentrated on a succession of small pots and continued their noisy altercations that were fired up by the big jug of whiskey.

But, as Caroline Chauvin was to discover, the appearance of drunkenness can be deceptive and its degree is often closely associated to mood and occasion.

The bullet fired at Caroline by Jake Hustler as Alice LaClaire and Dom Ramés were making their escape had knocked her sideways, but had been harmlessly deflected by the thick leather of the belt around her slim waist. She had been badly winded, would be sore for days, would breathe with great care and was expecting to see a wonderful purpling bruise when she lifted her shirt.

But nothing, she swore softly yet vehemently, would prevent her from going after the man she had been patiently seeking for the past six months – and had now found.

Immediately after the escape, Wilson and the poker players had helped get the injured men back inside the station. The coach-driver's lower leg was broken. Jake Hustler had a flesh wound in the left shoulder and an ugly look on his face every time he stared at Caroline Chauvin.

The marshal's intention was to take her on to Topeka. His pride had been badly dented; one prisoner delivered to the capital was better than three on the loose.

But, as Caroline knew full well, the federal lawman was facing difficulties. He had no driver. His injured shoulder was a handicap. He could try to hire one of the poker players as temporary driver – but Caroline was sure they'd laugh in his face. Or he could return to Coffeyville. That, too, meant a long drive sitting upright clinging to traces with Caroline likely at any time to make a break for freedom.

Stark choices. But whatever he decided, Hustler was unlikely to make a move until the next morning.

Caroline had other ideas.

After a while the excitement died down. The coach driver's leg had been splinted and strapped. Hustler was again at the bar, talking and drinking with Wilson – after making sure the door and all windows were secure.

The poker players were again sitting at the long table, but the deck of cards had been put to one side and they were quietly smoking and talking. Risking a warning glance from Hustler, Caroline went to join them. She slid into a seat alongside the biggest and hairiest, grabbed a glass and helped herself to a splash of whiskey.

It nearly blew off the top of her head.

Grins all round. She gasped, wiped her eyes and her mouth, then leaned forward and urged the three men close.

'I've got to get out of here,' she said softly.

'Ain't nowhere to go,' the hairy one said bluntly.

'Your pals stole two of our horses,' said a man with a scarred cheek. 'You think we'd hand over the third?'

'Yes. If I've got good enough reason.'

The men exchanged glances. A little pipsqueak with a wall eye shrugged.

'Keep talking,' he said, in a voice too deep for his frame.

'Six months ago, a man murdered my grandparents.'

'New Orleans,' the hairy one said, then grinned sheepishly at his comrades. 'I read the papers.'

'For the past six months I've been riding north with a group—'

'Bank robbers.'

'That's the way we turned out. Point is, one of that group – a man I like very much – is wanted for that double murder down in New Orleans. If he did it, circumstances put the weight of blame firmly on my shoulders – don't bother asking me why. Anyhow, while riding north I've been biding my time, keeping my eyes and ears open, hoping for some sign, something that proves beyond doubt that he's guilty, or he's not. Tonight I got that sign. The man called Boudreaux didn't do it, because I've found the real killer.'

The man with the scar frowned. 'You found him here?'

'I knew what he looked like. Sort of. I saw him running away minutes after he'd . . . he'd murdered my folk. But it was a dark night. Raining. I couldn't identify him, couldn't say for sure if it was Boudreaux or not, couldn't even be sure I'd recognize him if I saw him again.'

'So what changed?' said the man with the straggly beard.

'I saw him tonight exactly as he was then—'

'Couldn't have done. It's not raining, there's a moon.'

Caroline flapped an impatient hand, then winced and rubbed her side.

'You know what I mean. Anyway, the moonlight made it easier. I was looking towards the corral when my companions were making their break and I got a clear view—'

'One of them?' Pipsqueak said, startled.

'The man in black. I don't like him, but I've never suspected him. He was probably dressed in black that night in New Orleans, but the darkness made it impossible to tell. Here, I didn't need to look at his black clothing. What I saw when he went for that third horse—'

'*My* horse,' the man with the scar growled.

'What I saw,' Caroline went on, glaring, 'was a man running sort of stooped over and in his hand a knife was flashing. Tonight he was about to cut a cinch. That night

136

six months ago he'd just finished slicing two defenceless throats. They belonged to my grandma and my grandpa.'

There were collective hisses of indrawn breaths.

'You're sure?'

That was Scarface. Caroline nodded.

'Near as dammit. When I get to him – if you'll allow me to do that – there's one way I can find out for certain.'

'How?'

'Don't let it worry you.' Caroline looked at the three men. 'So, what do you say? Do you help me?'

The bearded one was grinning.

'We watched you use feminine charm to wrap that federal man around your dainty little finger. What d'you suggest I should do?'

'Well, you are the biggest,' Caroline said. 'Why don't you just go across there and put the marshal in an arm lock?'

'Be a pleasure.'

'However,' Caroline said, 'there is one problem – two, I suppose.' She looked at the man with a scar. 'I do need that horse, and last time I looked a killer was ruining the saddle.'

'There's saddles in the shed at the end of the building,' he said. 'I'll go fix up your mount.'

After that it was all too easy.

The hairy man strolled over to the bar, had a few words with the wounded Jake Hustler and it turned out an arm lock wasn't necessary. While the big man was keeping the marshal in place with a friendly arm around his wounded shoulder, Pipsqueak escorted Caroline out of the building. Scarface had saddled her horse.

It was Scarface, too, who unstrapped his gunbelt and buckled it, complete with holster containing a big Smith & Wesson Schofield .45, around Caroline's slender waist.

'Just so's I can be sure of seeing you again soon,' he said with a broad wink.

Less than ten minutes after appealing for help, Caroline Chauvin was out on the trail and eating up the miles to the hollow.

EIGHTEEN

A short way into the ride to the hollow, Gatlin and Pine decided that Ramés and Tom Bellard should take the lead. It made sense for two reasons: both the men leading the way would know exactly where they were heading and, exposed at the head of the group, it would be more difficult for the desperate Ramés to make a break and get the jump on them.

The spot where Ramés had marked the trail with a white blaze, and where the stolen money had apparently changed hands a couple of times, was roughly halfway between Coffeyville and their destination. It left the quartet with some ten miles to cover. They made it in under an hour.

As they neared the end of the ride, Bellard held his hand up in warning, and the four came together.

'I know this place well. In this moonlight, anyone watching from deep in the hollow will easily pick out a rider on the skyline.'

'Or pick 'em *off* – with a rifle,' Pine said.

Bellard nodded. 'My thoughts exactly, so here's what I

suggest. There are trails down through the mesquite at the north and south ends. I'll take Ramés around to the north, block that way out. When we're in position' – he grinned somewhat bashfully – 'well, I can make a pretty fair imitation of a coyote.'

'We'll look forward to it,' Gatlin said with an answering smile. 'Just thank the Lord it's not the mating season.'

'Pierre?' Alice LaClaire called softly.

'Stay down. Keep out of sight, use the trees as cover.'

'Can you see anything? Any riders?'

'Not yet.'

'Listen, I've thought of something. Almost as good as your idea of trying to rob a bank.'

'Yeah,' Boudreaux said with deep irony, 'now that was a *real* good idea, because look where it's got us.'

He had positioned himself on the edge of the trees and was able to see north and south. He was hunkered down. A Winchester was in his right hand, the butt resting on the damp grass. Even while talking his eyes were constantly searching the skyline, looking for movement. So far all he'd got was a dull ache behind his eyes from staring too hard into the distance.

'We know there's two ways into the hollow, down those mesquite trails that tear half the skin off your bones, and we can't use those.' Alice said. 'But what about the river? That flows in one end, flows out the other. I've been looking around, and there's plenty of fallen timber here. Couldn't we sort of use some of that to float downstream?'

Boudreaux chuckled. 'That thought crossed my mind a half-hour ago. Then I thought of us out there on the water, two sitting ducks.'

'But wouldn't they just think it was a couple of old logs—?'

'What was that?'

Alice frowned. 'Sounded like a . . . a coyote?'

'To me,' Boudreaux said, 'it sounded much more like some feller trying to *play* coyote. And as there's no Injuns out there, then I guess those fellers up there have got themselves organized and are about to move in.'

'Before he rode off with Ramés,' Gatlin said, 'I told Tom he's to do a holding job. If Boudreaux and whoever's down there with him try to get out that way, stop them, otherwise do nothing. If we do well and manage to get our hands on those two bank robbers, I told Tom we'll holler, call him down.'

'So it's down to the Pinkertons again,' Charlie Pine said.

'Who better to do the job?' Gatlin said.

'True, but I'd be happier if it was us holding Ramés. Tom's an easy-going sort of fellow, and I don't trust that bank-robbing son of a gun one bit.'

Even as the Pinkerton man finished speaking they both heard the plaintive call of a coyote.

'That's it,' Gatlin said. 'Tom's in position. Trouble is, if we can hear that call, so can Boudreaux. Let's hope it was good enough to fool him.'

Without another word he pointed his horse towards the mesquite that tumbled down in a grey-green wave towards the floor of the hollow where the moonlit Elk River could be seen as a silver ribbon curling away towards the glow of a camp-fire.

141

'First time we've been close enough to the edge to get a sight of that fire,' Gatlin said over his shoulder. 'Least we now know where they're located.'

'Yeah, and it's the first time we've been on the skyline with the moon at our backs so Boudreaux can draw a bead on us,' Pine warned.

But Gatlin was away. He had already eased his horse over the lip and was commencing to work his way down through the tangle of branches and thorns that at once began tearing at his pants and gloved hands.

The shot, when it came, whistled over his head. It was followed by the crack of the powerful rifle and, behind him, the solid thwack as the bullet struck home. Cursing, knowing Boudreaux had recognized the coyote call for what it was and been put on the alert, he twisted in the saddle to look back.

Pine had been following him. Clearly the gunman down in the hollow had spotted both men as soon as they appeared on the skyline. His reactions had been a mite slow. By the time he had steadied, taken aim and squeezed the trigger, Gatlin had dropped out of sight. Instead of taking Gatlin, that first slug dropped Pine's horse.

Pine was already scrambling to his feet. He wrenched his rifle from the boot trapped under the fallen horse, unbuckled his saddle-bags and slung them over his shoulder, then waved Gatlin on.

'I'll follow on foot,' he called. 'You'll be slow enough going down. At the bottom we can ride double.'

Gatlin lifted a hand in acknowledgement, and again turned to the trail. As the jolting of the horse's difficult descent jarred his bones and rattled his teeth he found himself wondering just how much Boudreaux was able to see from the campsite. All right the light was poor, the camp-fire was a good quarter mile away and Gatlin was riding through thick scrub that was effective cover, but there would surely be sections were the growth thinned and a rider would be visible from afar.

The answer to his question came quickly. A bullet snicked through the taller mesquite and plucked at his sleeve. The crack that followed brought his mount's head up and made Gatlin duck instinctively and grab for the horse's mane. That reaction brought a rueful smile to his face and a comment from Pine, stumbling down the trail some yards behind him.

'That did about as much good as scrunching up your shoulders in a rainstorm to keep from getting wet.'

'We all do it,' Gatlin said, gritting his teeth.

Shoulders crawling, scalp prickling, he plunged on down the trail. Gradually the slope eased and, as he drew closer to the grassy floor of the hollow, the vegetation became lush and almost impenetrable. Boudreaux was once more unsighted. There were no more shots.

But now, as Gatlin emerged from the mesquite, he knew that their troubles had just begun. Boudreaux had been content to let them work their way down through the thick undergrowth – with the occasional shot to keep them on their toes – because from now on he knew they would be riding across open ground. The moon was at their backs, turning them into black cut-outs outlined against luminous skies. Boudreaux had doused the camp-fire. He was lost in the shadows under the trees, waiting to pick them off.

As Gatlin sat in the saddle gazing out across the hollow and gloomily assessing their chances, a breathless Pine caught up with him. He dropped the saddle-bags and hung onto Gatlin's saddle horn.

'You're out of condition,' Gatlin said.

'Yeah, and we should've come up with a workable plan at the start,' Pine panted. 'Now's the time we need Tom making loud noises at the far end of the hollow, drawing Boudreaux's attention while we move in. Instead, he's all tied up with Ramés and doing that simple holding job.'

'My fault,' Gatlin said.

'But up to us both to put it right.'

'Yes. And right now it seems Boudreaux's holding all the cards.'

'You're talking nonsense, Jim. The man's trapped.'

'In a way, so are we. Riding across open ground would be suicide. We know where he is – he's now less than four hundred yards away – but we can't get near him.'

'You think not? Look at it this way – if he could reach us when we were coming down that trail, then sure as hell we can reach him now.'

'Using rifles, you mean?' Gatlin's nodded quickly. 'How're you fixed for cartridges?'

Pine kicked the saddle-bags. 'I'm not toting that lot for fun. There's enough in here for both of us to hold off an army – or make a certain bank-robber and his young woman mighty uncomfortable.'

'I noticed a side trail on the way down,' Gatlin said thoughtfully. 'Some massive rocky outcrops. If we go back fifty yards we'll have the advantage of elevation, and cover.'

'All right for you,' Charlie Pine said plaintively, 'but you know how I hate walking.'

'What are they doing?'

Alice LaClaire's voice was a whisper in the darkness.

'Nothing. They made it all the way down the trail. Now they're wondering what they've got themselves into.'

'So am I. We spent too much time talking instead of riding.'

There was a long silence. Boudreaux shifted his position. The rifle barrel glittered. He stood up and kicked earth over the fire's remaining glowing embers. Then he walked over to Alice. Her hair was a golden glint in the darkness.

'If we offered to return the money,' she said softly, 'that would do some good, wouldn't it?'

'I don't know.'

'But isn't that what Dom was going to do, when he had it?'

'Dom's done what he was going to do – he's betrayed us.'

'Then isn't that the end of it? What's the use in going on—'

She broke off and stood in stunned silence as two rifles opened up from across the hollow. They could both see the muzzle flashes, bursts of angry red light a little way up the distant mesquite slope. Around them bullets began tearing through the trees. Leaves fluttered to the damp earth. Splinters, sharp and white, flew from the trees.

'They saw the fire, that's why those shots are coming too damn close,' Boudreaux said. He was down on one knee, rifle to his shoulder. His eyes were narrowed as he

145

concentrated on the distant riflemen. 'It's no longer safe here under the trees, Alice. Move yourself.'

As rifle fire continued to pour in, Boudreaux moved along the outer fringes of the small wood, found a convenient boulder and began to return fire. His targets were the muzzle flashes. He fired steadily, aiming at one, then the other. His intention was to keep the men's heads down; hope that he got lucky, did more than that, managed to down one or both of them.

If they didn't get him first.

There was a sudden lull. In the tense calm, Boudreaux remembered Alice. He'd told her to move – but where had she gone?

Then he saw her. He'd told her it wasn't safe under the trees, and she'd taken that warning literally. She was standing in the open, down by the river; must have been standing watching as Boudreaux and the gunmen on the slope exchanged shots, happy to be well out of the line of fire.

Then one of the distant rifles opened up again. For an instant Boudreaux was confused. Then he realized what was wrong. No bullets were snicking through the trees, kicking up dirt close to the camp-fire, drawing sparks from the boulder behind which he was sheltering.

This time, Alice was the target.

Boudreaux's hair prickled.

'Jesus Christ, no, no!' he roared. He sprang to his feet, waved the rifle over his head, ran from the trees. 'Alice, for God's sake get down, they're firing at *you*—'

And then he stopped.

There had been the soft, meaty sound of a bullet hitting

flesh. Alice LaClaire seemed to half turn, to look at him.

Then, without a sound, she crumpled to the grassy bank and lay still.

NINETEEN

Charlie Pine was cursing softly.

'I saw a figure move out of the trees and down to the river. I fired a shot intended to drive whoever it was closer to the water, move the two bank robbers even further apart. Then I saw my shot had gone astray. I saw it hit home, saw the long blonde hair when the figure went down and I knew I'd hit a woman.'

He was hanging on to Gatlin's belt, talking heatedly to the back of his partner's neck as they rode double along the river bank. Ahead of them they could see the crumpled shape down in the grass, the figure kneeling alongside her.

'They both knew the risks they were taking,' Gatlin said. 'Those risks began the minute they rode into Coffeyville and pulled a gun on the manager of the First National bank. After that kind of stupidity, it's inevitable that sooner or later there'd be a posse and bullets are going to start flying.'

It took no more than a minute for the two Pinkerton men to cover the 400 yards to the campsite. Gatlin drew rein, hauled the horse to a halt. Both men tumbled from the horse and ran to the downed woman.

'She's alive,' Boudreaux said, his face pale as he looked up. 'She took the slug in her shoulder and she's out cold. We need to get her to a doctor.'

'You should have thought of that—'

'Damn it, Alice is my half sister, now's not the time—'

'Shut up. You're Jean Pierre Boudreaux – is that right?'

Boudreaux nodded numbly. He was watching Charlie Pine, who had dropped to his knees alongside the wounded woman and roughly pushed Boudreaux out of the way. The Pinkerton man pulled up the dark skirt, tore a strip from the white under slip and folded it into a pad which he slipped inside the top of the young woman's bodice and pressed against the bloody wound.

'Let's get this straight,' Gatlin said. 'The young woman is Alice LaClaire. Caroline Chauvin took a slug that probably finished her when LaClaire and Ramés were escaping from Wilson's station. Dom Ramés is up there with Deputy Tom Bellard, so it seems all four of you are accounted for.'

'Ramés led you here?'

Gatlin nodded. 'He gave us this location.'

'Buying his freedom. But this is not all about a bank robbery, is it? You're after me for the New Orleans murders.'

'Maybe.'

Boudreaux gaped. '*Maybe?* What the hell does that mean?'

'It means a new witness has come forward, and there's some doubt about your guilt.'

'Oh my God,' Boudreaux breathed softly.

'All that can wait,' Gatlin said. 'We'll get Tom Bellard down here, then see about getting LaClaire into Coffeyville.'

With the young woman's wound covered by a temporary dressing, Pine had stood up and walked a little way away from LaClaire. Now he lifted both hands to his mouth and his loud cry rang out, echoing in the still air.

There was no reply.

Pine called again.

Then, out of the aching silence above them all three men heard the sound of a single horse's hoofs, receding into the distance.

The Pinkerton men exchanged glances.

'Dammit, I told you I didn't trust that man,' Pine said.

'Whatever he did to Bellard, he did quietly,' Gatlin said. 'He carries a knife.'

It was Alice LaClaire who had spoken. Her voice was weak, but clear. She was half sitting, supported by Boudreaux's arm around her shoulders.

'Dom always has it in his boot,' LaClaire said. 'I saw him use it to cut a saddle cinch at Wilson's station.'

'He must use it with some skill,' Gatlin said, 'to have overpowered Tom Bellard.'

'He won't get far,' Pine said. 'I can use Boudreaux's horse—'

Boudreaux shook his head. 'My horse is lame.'

'Take mine,' Alice said. 'It's an old nag from Wilson's station, but it's fresh.'

'But what about Alice?' Boudreaux said.

She grasped his hand. 'I'm fine, Pierre. If Dom's done

something really bad they must go after him, you know that.'

'We're wasting time,' Pine said bluntly.

Gatlin lifted a hand in acknowledgement, then looked hard at Boudreaux.

'Ramés buried the money. When he took us to the spot, it had gone.'

Boudreaux nodded. 'I was watching him.'

'So you've got it?'

Again Boudreaux nodded.

'All right. You've got the money, and we're forced to leave you here with it. But I'd like you to think hard on what I told you. There's a possibility you'll be cleared of any involvement in the New Orleans murders. If the money's returned, the Coffeyville raid's going to look a lot less serious. Don't blow those chances, Boudreaux—'

'For Christ's sake, will you look at us?' Boudreaux blurted angrily. 'We've got one lame horse between us. Because of my bright ideas, Alice is in no shape to stand, never mind ride, and no money in the whole of the West can change that, turn the clock back. . . .'

But he was talking to Gatlin's back. The Pinkerton man was running to his horse.

Already mounted, Pine said, tongue in cheek, 'I'm likely to get ahead of you, because Alice's horse has been rested some. Could be it'll all be over by the time you catch up.'

'I'm not counting on it,' Gatlin said with a grim smile. 'And you'd be wise to bear this in mind – if Ramés has got away from Bellard he'll now be armed with a six-gun, and doubly dangerous.'

*

They found Tom Bellard a short way from the top of the twisting track through the mesquite that took them out of the north end of the hollow. He was lying on his back, half hidden in the undergrowth. His throat had been cut. His shirt front was soaked in blood. A few yards away his horse was bolt upright, ears pricked, the whites of its eyes showing.

'Goddammit,' Gatlin said quietly, his hands soothing his own mount as it tried to back away from the smell of fresh blood. 'What kind of a man would do something like that?'

He was watching Pine, who was again off his horse and down on his knees alongside a warm body.

But this one was dead.

Pensively, Gatlin said, 'Could be I can answer my own question about the kind of man who kills by slitting throats. And maybe you're getting the same idea I'm getting.'

'The idea I'm getting is there's nothing we can do for Bellard, so any talk here is time wasted,' Pine said. He had wiped his bloodstained hands on the grass, and was remounting. 'Let's get after Ramés, Jim, and figure out just what kind of an animal we've roped when the job's done.'

The moon was still high enough to cast its pale light over the landscape. A quick look around told the two Pinkerton men that the scrub around the rim of the hollow spread outwards for miles in all directions except north, and was in many places almost impenetrable. A man in a hurry was left with only one option: ride north; and Ramés was desperate.

The trail north was broad, meandering, hard-packed and well lit. As Charlie Pine had predicted, mounted on Alice's rested horse he would have the edge over Gatlin. So it proved. Within a mile of furious riding he was a hundred yards ahead and pulling away. Another mile and he was out of sight around one of the sweeping bends and Gatlin, forced to ease his weary horse back to a steady canter, was gritting his teeth in frustration.

He rode like that for a further ten minutes, feeling the gallant animal struggling beneath him, hearing the harsh sound of its breathing and, up ahead, the distant and ever-fading drum of hoofs as Alice's horse continued to pull away from him.

Then, above all those sounds, he heard the crack of a shot. It was a deep, barking cough. Not a rifle. A heavy six-gun. Charlie Pine carried a Remington .44. Tom Bellard, Gatlin recalled, favoured a Colt Navy .36. Both weapons were comparative lightweights.

With foreboding settling heavily on his shoulders, Jim Gatlin pushed on. He covered another mile, no more than that. Then, ahead of him there was another bend, this one tighter and flanked on both sides by stands of trees that cast dark shadows across the trail.

Dom Ramés was in the centre of the trail. He was sitting stiff in the saddle. His hands were raised, level with his shoulders. Behind him, thirty yards back and much closer to Gatlin, Charlie Pine was doing nothing but watch.

Twenty yards beyond both of them, a dark-haired young woman mounted on a ragged pony was pointing a big pistol at Ramés. She was sitting awkwardly in the saddle, as if suffering acute pain. Which was probably true, Gatlin thought; this must be Caroline Chauvin, the young woman who had taken a bullet at Wilson's station and, confounding all reports, had come out of that gunfight alive.

Alive, and dangerous enough to start one of her own, Gatlin thought, easing his tired horse towards the group. Also, it was possible that six months ago in New Orleans she had committed murder.

But what was this all about?

'Damn near shot him out of the saddle,' Charlie Pine said, not taking his attention from the young woman as Gatlin drew alongside. 'Ramés has been asking her what the hell's going on. She said something about recognizing him – whatever the hell that means—'

He broke off. The young woman had ridden closer to Ramés. She was waggling the big six-gun. Her face was pale, her eyes hot.

'Recognized you in New Orleans,' she said. '*That's* what I mean.'

'We *met* in New Orleans—'

'Before that. One dark, wet night. I saw a man running. Lean as a racing hound. Carrying a knife. If I'd been closer I'd have seen bloodstains, right, Dom? Because that man was you.'

'What the hell are you trying to pin on me? These are Pinkerton men, are you aware of that? And it was Boudreaux murdered that old couple, they know it and they've been hunting him.'

'What old couple?' Caroline smiled sweetly, her

154

eyebrows raised. 'Do you mean my grandparents?'

Ramés flinched.

'These men told me all about it,' he protested. 'And I can read newspapers. Boudreaux's on the run for murdering two people in an apartment on Bourbon Street. Hell, you're forgetting, we already knew that because it's the reason we all headed north.'

'Boudreaux decided to head north because he couldn't see how he could clear his name. True. But you tagged on because you were also in trouble. You never told us the details, did you?'

'It was nothing—'

'I saw you that night, with a knife. It was you, wasn't it?'

'No—'

'What's that you wear around your neck, Dom?'

'Wha—?'

'Suspended from that leather thong you're always playing with. Pull it out, now, let's all see what's there.'

'It's something was given to me by my mother.'

'Pull it out, Ramés.'

Gatlin had ridden forward. He stopped with the bank robber on his right side. Caroline Chauvin had also moved closer. Charlie Pine stayed put.

Ramés was shaking his head. Beneath his hat brim his forehead was glistening.

'I told you—'

'When those old folk were murdered,' Gatlin said, 'an amulet was stolen. The old man had brought it with him from Russia. Now, I don't believe in coincidence. I don't think your mother was Russian. So, if what you're wearing around your neck turns out to be—'

155

Metal flashed as Dom Ramés spun in the saddle. He had been holding a bone-handled knife flat against his left wrist. Using a backhand throw he flipped the blade at Gatlin. The knife spun, flashing in the moonlight. The razor-sharp metal sank into the flesh of the Pinkerton man's shoulder. Liquid fire shot down his arm. His hand went numb.

In the same twisting movement, Ramés drew his six-gun with his right hand. His left arm was still extended from the throw that had crippled Gatlin. He fired under that arm and blew Charlie Pine out of the saddle.

Then he raked his horse with spurs and drove it straight at Caroline Chauvin.

It was a waste of effort that got him nowhere.

Gatlin was bent over in the saddle. His right arm was held rigidly straight. His numb right hand was on the saddle horn. With his trembling left hand he grasped the slippery bone hilt of the knife. When he clenched his teeth and tried to pull the blade from his flesh, everything swam before him. He was a man looking at a blurred world from beneath the surface of a warm lake, every second sinking deeper.

Out of those shimmering depths he watched Dom Ramés drive his horse at Caroline Chauvin. The bank robber had knifed one man, shot another and yet he chose to use brute force against the woman. Maybe he thought she was fragile, Gatlin thought wildly. Or maybe, while arguing with her, he had planned the sequence of events that would bring him his freedom and was locked into that pattern: knife, shoot, ride down.

Coolly, the dark-haired young woman shot Ramés

156

between the eyes. She was using, Gatlin learnt later, a borrowed Smith & Wesson Schofield. The powerful slug drilled into Ramés's head and removed the back of his skull. His hat flew off in a shower of blood and bone. He went sideways off his horse. His dead body slammed against Caroline's thigh as his horse swerved to avoid the collision.

Dom Ramés flopped onto his back on the hard trail. That final, dying movement that preceded eternal stillness disturbed the rawhide thong that hung loose around his throat. From the opening at the neck of his shirt an amulet slid free. It was oval, and quite small, but in the fading moonlight it gleamed like a precious jewel. The richness of its red, yellow and gold enamels caught and reflected the last of the moon's waning light.

'There's my answer,' Caroline Chauvin. 'Mine, and yours, Pinkerton man, because now everyone knows the identity of the man who murdered my grandparents in New Orleans.'

Gatlin shuddered. One final tug and the knife had come free. He let it fall to the ground. He followed it with his eyes, then looked up. His vision had cleared. Charlie Pine was limping towards him. Jim Gatlin knew, with a feeling of intense exhilaration, that both of them had come through once again, bloody but undefeated.

'I guess this calls for a wire to Jim McParland up in Denver,' Pine said hoarsely.

'When I'm ready for more of his sick jokes, I'll send a wire,' Gatlin agreed. 'In the meantime, and before I fall out of this saddle, there's a lot of clearing up to be done between here and Coffeyville.'

'That clearing up,' Pine said, 'will have to be done without a certain young woman.'

Like a dark shadow, and as suddenly as she had appeared, Caroline Chauvin had disappeared into the night.